Thunder in the Heartland

Parables from Oklahoma

By Jim Marion Etter

NEW
FORUMS

Stillwater, Oklahoma
U.S.A.

This book may be ordered in bulk quantities at discount from
New Forums Press, Inc., P.O. Box 876, Stillwater, OK 74076
[Federal I.D. No. 73 1123239]. Printed in the United States of
America.

ISBN 10: 1-58107-155-8
ISBN 13: 978-1-581071-55-9

Second paperback edition / 2 3 4 5 6 7 8 9 0

To every Oklahoman I've ever
met, plus a few other folks.

Contents

Foreword

If you're an Oklahoman, like I am, I bet you'll like this book as much as I do. And if you're from anywhere else in this great nation, or even from Timbuktu, chances are you'll still like it.

It's a book about people. People of long ago, when this was the Old West, and people who live here now. People in the middle of America, when Oklahoma, and the whole country, was growing up. It's about good people and bad people, and the kind of people you and I know: everyday people.

This is fiction with just the right amount of fact. Every story has a dab of true history, and a whole lot of flavor. The flavor of Oklahoma, and the flavor of America.

I think you'll agree these stories are like real life: They can make you proud, make you laugh, and maybe even make you cry.

Some of them remind me of a television series I used to like. I bet a lot of you liked it, too. It was called "Wells Fargo."

Dale Robertson,
Actor and Screenwriter

About the Author

JIM MARION ETTER grew up during the 1930s and '40s in the small eastern Oklahoma community of Oktaha, where he dreamed of becoming a writer while riding horses, fishing and hunting, and reading the funny papers.

He began his writing career with *The Muskogee Daily Phoenix & Times-Democrat* in Muskogee, spent several years as a reporter in Laredo, Texas, and retired after some 20 years on the news staff of *The Daily Oklahoman*. He also served as a reserve military journalist in Latin America.

His other books include "WHAT A DIRTY SHAME! 100 Unforgettable Place Names of Oklahoma"; "Ghost-Town Tales of Oklahoma – Unforgettable Stories of Nearly Forgotten Places"; "Between Me & You & The Gatepost – Rural Expressions of Oklahoma" (two editions); "Oktaha, A Track in the Sand"; and "The Grains of Time," a history of the Oklahoma Grain and Feed Association. He is among the authors in such anthologies as "Daughters of the Land"; "The Salt of the Earth"; "Western Horse Tales"; "New Trails – 23 Original Stories of the West"; and "Black Hats." His work has been published in several magazines including *Persimmon Hill, Western Horseman, American Cowboy, Desert Exposure, True West, Western Digest, Country Discoveries, Route 66, Oklahoma Today* and *ByLine*.

www.jimetter.com

The 'Heartland' Tales

Just as truth can be stranger than fiction, sometimes it takes a touch of fable to give a true story the luster of immortality.

The following tales inspired by fact, including the portrayal of a monumental tragedy a dozen years before Oklahoma's centennial, are glances back at a few happenings, circumstances and traditions that are the soul of the Sooner State.

This book is also aimed at clearing up a hazy image.

The state's history bulges with such vital and rousing topics as American Indians, cowboys, land runs, the vitality of Jim Thorpe, the enduring philosophy of Will Rogers, and the grit of poor Okies who once rattled westward on Route 66.

But the place is spoken of as Western, Southern and Midwestern, and as both a plains country and a backwoods – and by travelers as a blur of pastoral countrysides, green wheat pastures, and a land of church steeples, football fans and big belt buckles.

It is hoped these stories will show the state is in a category of its own – one that is purely *Oklahoma*.

The Author

Thunder in the Heartland

This story is inspired by the life of Millie Durgan, who as a baby was taken in an 1864 Indian raid on North Texas settlers, and raised by the Kiowas as Sain-toh-oodle (Killed With Blunt Arrow). She was devoted to her adoptive parents, married into the tribe, lived all her days as a Kiowa, and in her heart was never anything else. She was also known as Mrs. Goombi. Her great-grandson, J.T. Goombi of Anadarko, in the late 1980s and early '90s was tribal chairman. She is buried near Mountain View. Everything else in the following is fiction.

The Lost Kiowa

The dream had come again, clinging to her like a heavy robe, yet shadowy and fleeting like a wolf at dusk. Runs With Feather shuddered as she lay in the darkness, now awake, her thoughts mingling with the sound of the night wind caressing the outside of her family's lodge. And she wondered, as she always did, if the wispy visions that returned over and over to dance in her head were indeed a dream, bearing some grave message, or simply fragments of an actual, distant memory — one she wished she could completely forget.

There was fighting. She could taste the blood that seeped from around her teeth, clenched in fear; hear the war cries and the roar of the great weapons; and smell the sweaty anxiety of the warriors as they threw themselves against the white devils.

Next, she was alone — until she saw her mother in the distance. But her mother was someone she did not know. And as she tried to reach her, the strange, faceless woman began drifting away in the haze . . . .

Runs With Feather had long known she was white, and that the man and woman who raised her were not her birth parents — though she doubted it was possible to love or be loved by any two people more. Or, overall, to be happier. Her father, Big Bow, was respected as a warrior and a member of the tribe's councils, and she lived in a home with many warm skins and ample food. She always had good clothing and a fine pony. She had been taught and brought up well, and was proud to be a Kiowa.

But the dream haunted her. In spite of her comfort, and the fact she was treated like a princess — a name her father often called her — it left her feeling bewildered and frightened, like a young bird that had fallen from its nest.

She wished she were her parents' real child, and of their looks and color, and that she felt sure of their love.

Especially since a few other women referred to her as "that captive," and "the white one." These words left her hurt and angry, since she had proved herself to be a true Kiowa. She was able to skin animals, cook, make moccasins and clothing, and to ride, probably better than any young woman in the village — she could even hunt and knew that, if necessary, she could fight.

Such words were especially stinging to her because of her unusually benevolent attitude toward other members of the village. She had become known for her custom of visiting and offering kind words to the aged and sick. She often even accompanied the medicine man, Head of Buffalo, to the lodge of a very ill or dying person.

Among those who talked behind her back was Tall Lady, an older woman who wore a constant frown and had little good to say about anyone. Once, Runs With Feather overheard the old woman say to another that "the white captive should be with her own kind."

The remark pained her deeply — but also made her truly wonder about her kind. Were her birth father and mother gentle people, like her Kiowa parents? And were they now in the next world, which she envisioned as some great land high in the sky — perhaps smiling down upon her this very moment?

The remark also brought back the most disturbing part of her dream — that a voice was calling to her from some distant place. And with it came a strange yearning, a feeling of missing someone.

She often spoke of this to her mother, Smoldering Fire, while helping her gather berries, prepare game for stew or do other family chores.

"My mother, I know I have asked you this before, but the dream I have told you about — you don't believe it means

Millie Durgan, aka Sain-toh-oodle (Killed With Blunt Arrow) and Mrs. Goombi, in her later years. Western History Collections, University of Oklahoma Libraries.

something dreadful in my future, do you? And it ... It doesn't mean that you and my father don't really love me, does it?"

Her mother wrinkled her brow, but her words were patient and soothing. "Runs With Feather, like your father and I have told you many times, you are a perfect daughter. You have made us very proud of you, and we love you more than we could love anyone. You should ignore the dream, just as you should ignore the few others who gossip about you, as they are jealous of your beauty and status.

"Also, you will soon be at the age to marry and start a family of your own. Therefore, you must forget this silly dream, and think only of the future. Then you will have a bright one."

Runs With Feather felt herself blush, realizing her mother was aware of the quick, shy smiles between her daughter and Hunting Horse during ceremonial dances and other gatherings. He was handsome and mannerly and one of the most esteemed young men of the village.

Runs With Feather received similar counsel from Head of Buffalo, who, because of his position, she believed to be the wisest person in all her world. She also considered him one of her grandfathers, and took all his words to heart.

Head of Buffalo often frightened her by predicting that someday the Kiowas would lose the final battle with the whites, and those who survived would forever live in the shadow of the white man — but occasionally gave her more welcome words about herself. He told her that dreams, like a stream after much rain, often require time to clear, and that love between family members can be strong, without their being "of the same flesh."

He also told her, "Do not judge others too harshly, as you may not understand the reasons behind their actions. No person is perfect, as life itself is not perfect. You should think of this before judging."

She had assured him she did not feel harshly toward her father — to whom she felt sure he was referring, because of the way she was adopted.

It was a story her father had told her over and over, and one she loved to hear. She knew it by heart.

It was on a pleasant fall day many years ago when a band of warriors splashed their horses across the wide river to the south and into the land the white devils called Texas, to raid a scattered white settlement.

In one of the houses — following nearly a day of fighting, with arrows from the attackers and rifle bullets from both sides — Big Bow found five dead whites — apparently a man and his wife and three men who had served as workers. Before setting fire to the house, he heard a small whimper — which led him to find a baby girl hidden in a box beneath a portion of the floor. He instantly knew, as he held her up and looked into her frightened but beautiful gray-blue eyes, that this child was meant to be his.

"I said to you, 'Ahh, I will take you home with me, my lovely little princess. My wife is going to love you as I do. You will be our daughter forever and ever!' Seeing you for that first time was the most wonderful moment of my life. I will never forget it." With these words there always was a special glow of tenderness in his eyes.

As other captives were being taken by some of the raiders — mainly to be traded back to the whites for horses and other goods — Big Bow held the child with one arm as he galloped his horse back toward his home in the hills north of the river, forgetting the ugliness and bloodshed of the day's fighting and thinking only of the delightful surprise he had for his bride, Smoldering Fire.

They both adored the playful, happy child, and — though she was barely big enough to walk — named her because of her fondness for playing with feathers. Big Bow and his wife would have no other children — but would want no others.

Her father always became nervous when telling her about her birth parents being killed, as if he felt shame and worried about her feelings — though he explained that the attack was in retaliation for vicious acts by the whites, and that her mother, along with a few other women, had been killed, not intentionally, but in the heat of battle. It was the way of war.

Runs With Feather had been bothered about her real parents dying in such a way, but only for a short time — perhaps partly because of the way her father explained it, but mostly because to her, her Kiowa parents *were* her real parents. She wanted to think, as her father had led her to, that her birth mother and father were among the few innocent whites in this world; and that, as unwilling members of an evil species, their deaths had been a merciful design of some great, wise power.

Yet, regardless of the words from her parents and Head of Buffalo — who she knew always spoke true words — she continued to be bothered by her strange dream.

One night the dream was more vexing than ever — at least, she *thought* it was a dream. She had opened her eyes at dawn with an unsettling feeling. Perhaps the old dream had come to her in the night, but if so, it was more misty than before, and somehow different — and left her with the feeling that something bad was about to happen.

Later that day when she was carrying water from the creek, her mother called to her. A young boy had come with the message — Runs With Feather was needed; one of the older women in the village was very sick, and had asked for her. Head of Buffalo had already visited the woman; she had little time left.

Runs With Feather followed the boy, and found herself at the lodge of Tall Lady. Now the disturbing feeling covered her like the shadow of a giant owl — a fearful omen, she was sure.

As she stepped inside, the smell of death was thick. Soft moans came from the old woman. But Tall Lady's eyes found her, and brightened with recognition. An alert, even excited look came over the old woman's face and she began talking, her arms making jerky movements as if she wanted to pull Runs With Feather closer.

"I have a secret to tell you," she said, her voice halting but her words sharp. "Big Bow made me promise I would never tell, but now that I am soon to die I will no longer keep this to myself."

Runs With Feather felt her heart stop. Something in the old woman's eyes and voice told her she was about to hear some dreaded news — a truth that would be as hard to swallow as a sharp bone. She had always known this very moment would come, and she knew almost exactly Tall Lady's next words.

"Big Bow lied to you," she said. The old eyes gleamed, hatred replacing the look of pain, as she told Runs With Feather the very thing the girl did not want to believe — but somehow knew to be the truth: Her birth parents were not killed in the Kiowa raid. Instead, her birth mother, who lived in one of the white villages, gave her away.

Tall Lady said the woman was without a husband when she had a child, and made it known she wished to get rid of it. "Smoldering Fire had lost her new baby — it had been weak since its birth — and longed for another child. And Big Bow was desperate to find a child for her — any child."

Tall Lady caught her breath, then continued. "Your mother was not only white but was among the worst of the whites, one who would gladly throw aside her offspring — something that is never done even by the animals on the prairies. Even the other whites did not want the child. But Big Bow did. He lowered himself, and disgraced his own people. He took the white child."

The old eyes gleamed again. "Your mother was trash! And you — you are trash, like your white mother!"

"You lie, you evil old woman! You lie!" Runs With Feather heard her own words almost before she thought. Her hand gripped the handle of her skinning knife and she bolted toward Tall Lady's bed.

Tall Lady laughed — a cackle mingled with gasping and choking noises — and Runs With Feather tried not to hear more. She turned and ran, stumbling, from the lodge.

Afterward, Runs With Feather slipped into her bedding late, trying not to look at her parents, and lay in the darkness, her eyes filled with tears. She didn't know where she would go — the question bewildered her — but she knew this was the last night in what had long been her home. She could no longer feel as she once did within the tribe, could no longer face the other women of the village. And she could not feel worthy of any Kiowa man, especially Hunting Horse.

She would feel the same way among the whites. Even if she weren't the daughter of a shamed woman, she could not talk and act as they did. To them, regardless of her white looks, she would be a Kiowa squaw.

She had never felt more lost. She was like a tiny leaf drifting down from one of the great trees in the valleys.

She wished her birth parents had been killed as she was told at first, and which she had learned to accept. The beautiful story — the story upon which she had been nourished since childhood — was a shameful lie. Big Bow had made her live with a lie, then allowed her to be dishonored with the truth.

He was the only person left for her to love as her own — and she hated him.

The raid by the white dogface soldiers came in the darkness and chill of early morning. The many attackers swarmed down upon the sleeping village, shooting and slashing as their dreadful music played, leaving many dead. And while it brought flashes of the dream to Runs With Feather, the attack was worse than anything she had envisioned, either awake or asleep.

Finally, when the fighting was over and the sun was overhead, she remembered thrusting her skinning knife into a charging soldier, and escaping in the darkness. In her memory, which was still a fog, her parents somehow were far removed from the fighting, but she had lost contact with them when she fled with a few others — women and children, who scattered and hid until well after daylight.

She now trudged numbly along with them — all nearly

exhausted, weak from hunger, sick from the bloody outrage. They were in pain, if not from battle wounds, from the rocks and cactus that had torn their feet during their panicked flight in the darkness. On the long walk back toward their village, they also were in fear of what they would find.

But it all returned to her — the story about herself she had heard the day before. Regardless of how heavy her thoughts, the terrible raid by the white soldiers had swept them, though briefly, from her memory. If only she could forget forever.

It was early fall, and the weather was bright and still. On another day she would have savored the beauty, with the mesquite a pale green and the trees in the valleys now yellow, bright green and many shades of red. It was on such a day that, in her father's lovely story, he had taken her as his baby daughter.

The lie no longer made her hate him — but the sadness of it, which was worse than hate, clung to her. She believed it would always, like the paleness of her skin.

Runs With Feather trudged southward. For as disgusting and frightful was the thought of going to the whites, they were her people. Where the whites lived — that was her home.

She stopped on a bare rise. At a distance she could see the wide river. On the other side, she would find the white villages. Perhaps, because she was young, she would learn their language and other strange ways. Perhaps she would forget her own misplaced life and find a new one. Perhaps . . . .

It would take time - perhaps the rest of her life - to forget the ways of her past, and to cast away her memories.

They were good memories, most of them, of growing up with her Kiowa parents — of the way they taught her the family chores, the way her father taught her to ride, and other things she delighted in learning from him, such as how to recognize the many calls of the birds and other creatures. She recalled his many soft words and smiles. Even when he scolded her for some small mistake or act of mischief, there was the trace of amusement behind his words.

She wished she had told him how grateful she was for all of this, and how much she loved him.

She already missed him, and she knew now that she missed both him and Smoldering Fire far more than she ever imagined was possible. It was hard to think she would never see them again. Also, if she missed them this much already, even while they were still alive, how terribly she would miss them after they were gone. She would never stop missing them. She . . . .

While they were *still alive*?

It was then that the present came back to her — the raid! She and some others had escaped, but it could be the whole village was ravaged by the white devils, with many killed. It was as if she was jolted out of a trance, a period of insanity — and her heart pounded.

Tears blurred her vision as she ran back down the hill, her feet numb to the rocks and cactus. Her focus was now on one thing: find Big Bow and Smoldering Fire. If they were still to be found.

It was nearly sundown when Runs With Feather reached what was left of the village. She held her breath to keep from screaming as some of the few survivors told her of those killed — hearing the name of her mother, along with Head of Buffalo.

Her father was still alive, but mortally wounded. Hunting Horse was injured after waging a valiant fight, but would live.

She found Big Bow, and knelt at his side. He was still conscious. She was so glad for this — that she still had some time with him. She would not mention all that Tall Lady had told her.

"My father, please forgive me for not coming to you sooner. I ... I was far away for a time after the battle. I wandered toward the river because ... Because for a time I could not think clearly, and I . . . ."

Big Bow's hand grasped hers, and he slowly began to speak.

She looked away, tears of sorrow, but also of lingering resentment, in her eyes. She squeezed his hand in return.

"Tall Lady told you — I can tell by your voice." His words came between short breaths but his eyes were as keen as ever. "I thought Tall Lady would keep her promise not to tell you. But I should have known better. She was bitter — she lost a boy baby during a battle with the white devils. I am sorry I ... I am sorry I did not tell you myself."

He had difficulty speaking, but went on. "But I ... I must tell you everything. Tall Lady did not know all the story."

For Runs With Feather, time stopped and life stood still, as she forgot everything around her, everything that had happened, everything else she had heard this day. She listened without breathing.

Just after the raid on the white settlement, he learned from one of the captives that there was a place nearby where a white woman had a baby she wanted to give away. Smoldering Fire had just lost her baby girl, so he went to the place, guided by the captive in return for his release. Upon seeing the child, he happily agreed to take her, and brought the white baby home.

He said only a few people in the village, such as Tall Lady, knew the truth about her — and only a very few, such as Head of Buffalo, knew the *whole* truth.

"This woman who had this baby girl to give away, she ... She was what others called a whore — a woman who sold her body over and over to men."

"But you ... You must understand," he added. "She had to give her baby away because she was dying — she had an illness common among the whites that would not let her breathe without coughing. She loved the baby but had no choice. She gave her baby away so it could live. She . . . ."

Runs With Feather stopped him. "Why did you not tell me this to begin with? And why did you tell me you killed

---

my birth parents, knowing that could have made me hate you? If I had known the truth, I would have been grateful to you for saving me. And I would have . . . ."

It was then she thought of her life — except for some strange dreams and senseless gossip, a perfect one. She had felt proud to be a Kiowa.

She also thought of how her life would have been with the knowledge she had just been given — of how much worse her dreams, and how truly lost she would feel.

"You took a great risk, Big Bow! You made up this lie to protect me, as you have always protected me."

"It was all because I loved you, my daughter. We both loved you. Your mother and I agreed — it would be better to tell you the truth later, someday when you were grown. But as time passed, that no longer seemed important."

For Runs With Feather, the story of her life was now clear, like the cloudless sky on a clear fall day — a day in which silly dreams have no place. She would now turn all her thoughts to the future. And as the tribe regained strength and the village grew again, she would feel prouder each day to be the descendent of Big Bow and Smoldering Fire — even if sometime during her life she would see her people live in the shadow of the white man. Someday, she would tell her children about her great parents.

She wept, but held Big Bow's hand tightly and put her face close to his. "Thank you for everything you did, Big Bow, because I could not imagine growing up without you as my father. I will love you and my mother for the rest of my life — and I will still love you both when we are in the next world."

She thought for a moment. "And perhaps that world will be better. Better, perhaps, for all parents and children."

His eyes were now closed, but he smiled. Runs With Feather knew her father understood.

 *This is about the Chisholm Trail, one of Oklahoma's great legacies, and some of the land crossed by the famous Texas cattle route during the year 1880. In the author's imagination, it's also about a few of the people involved.*

A Drive for Santiago

"Whoa now, no need to get sassy!" Jess Cravens scowled through the dust from the cattle at the boy Chago, who was riding and looking off, the way he often did when Jess fussed at him. "I'm just tryin' to tell ya that you're gonna be better off bein' on your own hook."

Jess spurred Grasshopper, his tall, dun gelding, up a few jumps and slapped his coiled lariat at a brindle steer with a crooked horn that tried to dart into the mesquite. "After we sell these cows at Caldwell, we'll both be livin' high on the hog, and you'll have money in your pocket and be your own boss, too."

"I know, Jess. And I didn't mean to be sassy. I just meant that . . . Well, I don't need that much money, and why can't I just go back home with you?" Chago was riding Apple, a frisky little red bay that he kept holding back, partly because he was leading Pal, their packhorse.

Jess shook his head. "Boy, I wish you knew how much better off you're gonna be than I was at your age. Not makin' excuses, but I probably wouldn't have got in trouble with the law if it hadn't been for the way I grew up. Why, you ain't got no idy . . . ."

"I know, Jess, you've told me about that, a whole bunch of times."

"There you go again! Sometimes I have a good mind to drop you off somewhere without one dang *centavo!*"

Chago didn't answer, and looked off again. He was nearly seventeen, and had the brown eyes and olive hue of his mother, but a slightly large nose and other coarse Anglo features that made him somewhat homely – looking a little, oddly enough, like Jess.

For years Jess had hated being stuck with a son he didn't want – a situation that would be bad enough if the kid *were* his. But he knew he owed the boy something, too.

And now he had a plan to solve both problems.

He had been working for some time for R.J. McKenzie, a kindly old rancher in Texas who had let Jess build his own herd. Now he was taking his own twenty head – plus twenty of the rancher's cattle in exchange for his time off – to Red River Station to join a large drive bound for Kansas. Jess would split his part of the money with Chago — even if the boy, for some fool reason, didn't like the idea.

The sun was finally throwing long shadows of the riders and plodding cattle as they approached a small creek – and a good place to camp.

As soon as both had unsaddled, the steer with the crooked horn wheeled and went off in a long, high-tailed trot, heading back south.

"I shoulda butchered that ol' devil a long time ago," Jess said, and signaled to Chago to go after it.

"I'll be proud to go get 'im, Jess," the boy said, grinning, and swept up the reins, grabbed a strand of mane and swung onto the bay's sweaty back. And the young gelding was off in a high gallop through the scrubby willows.

Chago had taken to horses as soon as Jess pulled him up behind him and rode off from the *cantina* some twelve years ago, and learned to ride like a Comanche even quicker than he picked up Jess' brand of English. He could even walk up to any half-wild mustang and soon be riding it – bareback, with only a halter. And he could get the top speed out of any horse. He sat a horse light, plus somehow made it want to do its best.

Mr. McKenzie had been impressed, and gave Chago the little red horse when it was a colt. And probably the boy had never loved anything more.

Chago was back in a jiffy, the slobbering, cranky steer trotting ahead of him. "Here he is, Jess!" The boy's face shined with achievement.

"All right, but don't run the fat off of 'im!" Jess barked. "Even that ornery old steer's worth somethin', even if he probably *ain't* fit to eat."

Later, as both lay in their blankets, Chago asked him, "Jess, what was my mother like?"

"I've told ya before, she was just a nice lady. Now go to sleep."

Jess, an orphan, had been raised by an uncle and aunt with a passel of older, mean cousins on a rocky-hill farm in Arkansas.

Well after he was grown, he drifted into Texas, where he found honest work chasing cows – but not before he made the mistake of throwing in with two hard cases long enough to take part in a bungled holdup of a stagecoach. There was some shooting, and the three fled and split up. Jess hoped that was all it amounted to.

He made another big mistake one day when he stopped to have a drink on the Mexican border – and met Consuelo. She was so beautiful that he immediately forget what she was, and was soon under such a spell that he took her away with him.

After a few months, she left him to return to her more exciting life, while telling him she was pregnant — casually adding that it wasn't his. His simple arithmetic told him she was right, and he cursed himself for his child-like gullibility.

About five years later, he wandered back to the little

watering hole where he met her, and learned she had died, apparently of a sickness common within her profession.

And there was her son, the girls said. Jess saw a skinny, dirty-faced kid who shined boots and shoes and swiped change off the tables as men drunkenly frolicked with the bar women – the typical child of a *puta*. His name was Santiago – "Chago," the women called him.

That was when Jess – whether out of some strange sense of responsibility, or pure pity – made the decision that even at that moment he knew he would long regret.

"Jess," he heard Chago say, "what's Caldwell like?"

"Huh? Heck, I don't know. Nothin' to holler about, I guess."

"I was just thinkin', after we sell the cattle, and before I have to go on my own hook, reckon we can see the town? I mean, me and you see it together – you know, like I've heard you talk about with other men, 'raise a little hades'?"

"Shut up and go to sleep!" Jess said, then wished he hadn't said it like that. "We gotta be on the trail early."

Several days later, Jess and Chago were with the large drive after it had crossed into Indian Territory. Their cattle had been tallied and road-branded, and would be sold at Caldwell with the overall herd, with Jess to be paid then for the forty head. Jess was working as a regular hand, and Chago was helping the cook, plus serving as part-time nighthawk – a job the boy had wheedled by talking up his ability with horses.

Even the brindle steer with the crooked horn was adjusting, considering. It had brought both laughs and curses. It usually gave the drag riders fits by trying to head back to Texas, but other times was up front fighting the lead steer. And after the cook threw it some hard, leftover biscuits, it charged past the night guards once and nearly turned the wagon over.

The trail boss was J.T "Big John" Walker, one of the best in the business and known as a stern, but fair and decent man — even if it made Jess a little nervous that he was also considered a lawman. He had been a Texas Ranger, and occasionally did some investigating for the Stock Raisers Association of Northwest Texas.

Things were going well until a storm blew up.

It was a hot, still afternoon, and Jess was riding right swing and was some distance from the other drovers. He had been watching the pretty clouds – some of the fluffiest white shapes he had ever seen, floating against deep blue heavens – until they thickened into a dingy, gunmetal color and commenced to stir, covering the sun entirely.

The cattle became nervous. A cooling breeze swept up, turning the grass into pretty waves and swaying a family of sumac bushes and showing the light undersides of their leaves. The sweet smell of rain freshened the air, and a few drops fell – just as a jagged streak of lightning accompanied a deafening explosion that jarred the earth.

At the next crack of thunder the whole herd was in a scramble, drumming and sloshing through a beating rain that, between blinding flashes, had thrown the day into blackness and was soaking skin, hide and saddle leather. The world around Jess was filled with the bawling and ham-

A noon stop on the Chisholm Trail. Western History Collections, University of Oklahoma Libraries.

mering roar of hundreds of animals running in crazed blindness through sheets of water and slippery mud.

Jess, who was riding one of the remuda horses, tried to close in on part of the herd that was yawing to the right, but veered his mount to miss something just ahead – maybe a tumbleweed, a mesquite bush or a cedar scrub. The horse was tender-mouthed, and pulled around too short, and neither it nor Jess saw the arroyo soon enough.

When Jess opened his eyes he was lying in the shade of the chuck wagon. His back hurt – and hurt a lot worse when Chago and Big John Walker helped him stand up.

"You was the only one hurt in the stampede, Cravens," Walker said. "Even the horse is all right. But it looks like you're hurt aplenty. You won't be ridin' for a spell."

The trail boss said he would have to ride in the wagon, until they reached Darlington, probably the next day. There, they would have to leave him.

"That'll be a good place for you to mend," Walker said, explaining that Jess' forty head would be taken on to Kansas, and there cut out and penned, with instructions that he would be there later to sell his own cows. Walker would give him a signed paper showing that the forty head were his.

"I'm sorry, Cravens," he added, "but the cook needs the room in the wagon – he feeds a bunch of trail hands every day. And we got a herd to get to Caldwell."

Walker mounted his big buckskin and loped off, followed by another rider – a slender man with a spotted calfskin vest, on a tall chestnut horse with a fancy, California-style saddle. Jess realized the man had been hanging back, like he was listening, and he had an odd feeling about it – but figured it was because he had never seen such a fancy-looking trail hand.

Darlington, the Cheyenne and Arapaho Indian Agency near Fort Reno, was also a stage stop, post office, a supply station for cattle drovers, and even a community of sorts. Walker had given Jess a letter of introduction, which he showed to the agent, John D. Miles, who in turn directed him and Chago to the home of Mrs. Weatherford, a widow who kept boarders along with selling milk and eggs.

The room in the large, homey place was far better than the tiny hut where Jess and Chago lived on the Texas ranch. And Jess wouldn't even have to pay — Mrs. Weatherford said her hired hand had recently quit, so Chago, if he liked, could do the chores.

She was certainly fair, Jess observed, plus was the most ladylike and pleasant woman he had ever met, even if she talked funny, and was somewhat hefty, not to mention plain.

Over the next several days, Jess improved slightly, but still hurt too much to ride, and hated being supported by Chago's labor – even though Chago didn't seem to mind.

Besides caring for their own horses, he tended to the chickens and all the livestock, including milking three cows twice a day, and regularly cleaned the barn and henhouse. He also helped the blacksmith, who came often to work on Mrs. Weatherford's old buggy horse that was nearly crippled with bad feet. The boy worked like he was bucking for the job on a permanent basis.

And he probably was, and Jess knew the reason was Orna Mae, who helped Mrs. Weatherford in the kitchen. She was about Chago's age, and with clear blue eyes and long, shiny-clean hair the color of a honeycomb. At mealtimes, Chago lost interest in his food every time she whisked by, and when she smiled back, his ears turned purple.

The idea of Chago sniffing after the girl bothered Jess, as he had a feeling it would somehow further entangle his plans to put the kid on his own hook.

However, he forgot all that every time he had a conversation with Mrs. Weatherford – Hannah, he now called her. She was maybe ten years younger than him, and looked even younger when she smiled. She had pretty hazel eyes, and long brown hair with just enough gray to be fetching, especially when she wore it down – though that had shocked him at first – instead of in a bun, as she normally had. And her healthy body, though full, looked rounded just right under her long dresses, which showed her form better than the first one he had seen her wearing.

Also, her funny way of talking was now like clear Arkansas spring water flowing over pretty flint rocks. And he couldn't figure how he ever thought she was plain.

They often sat together on the front porch after dark, looking at the stars and listening to night birds and the little squeaks and cricks of insects, and visited. And while their backgrounds were vastly different, Jess was amazed they found so much to talk about.

She had come here from Ohio as the wife of an officer at Fort Reno, who soon afterward was killed in a training accident. Hannah, already a teacher by profession, taught part-time at the agency until she turned her home into a boarding house. She grew to like it here, and doubted she would ever return to the States.

Hannah also listened to Jess' troubles, and occasionally offered advice.

"Jess, about your . . . well, your first encounter with love. You're not the only person to make mistakes, and to feel regret." And she quoted a few lines from a poem that she said was written by someone named John Greenleaf Whittier:

For of all sad words of tongue or pen,
The saddest are these: "It might have been."

And about Chago, she said: "You know, I believe you see him as the symbol of a very bad time in your life — and haven't *looked* at him at all, and don't really know him. If you did, you'd know he wants to stay with you."

"Whoa now! You seem to have the idy I'm tryin' to get rid of that boy," Jess said. "True enough, he's been a bur under my saddle, but I'm tryin' to give 'im what I owe 'im — a good start on his own."

"But, Jess, he's been with you a long time, and probably what he really needs is you. After all, a child can be yours without – well, without really being *yours*."

One evening when Jess was helping Chago do the

chores, he learned that the boy and Orna Mae had been having similar conversations. She had told him a Bible story.

"Jess, you know what?" Chago spoke rapidly as he poured slop through the rails of the hog pen. "A long time ago there was a man, and his son took off and spent all the money he had on fool things – Orna Mae didn't say, but I guess it was whiskey and whores – and then came crawlin' back. And the father, instead of fussin' about it, just up and forgave 'im. He said it was time to rejoice because his son had come home, and he said they'd kill the fatted calf."

Jess was pleased Chago was learning things – but hoped they made sense, as he wasn't sure this one did to him.

After a few weeks, Jess figured he was barely able to ride – even if he didn't want to leave. He and Chago made plans to pull out the next morning.

That evening Jess and Hannah sat on the porch, and for the first time, talk wasn't coming easily between them.

"I hope you have a successful trip, Jess, and . . ." Her voice sounded strained. "And I hope you come back someday."

"I . . . I'd sure like to, Hannah. Maybe after I sell my cattle and then after I start another herd at the ranch in Texas . . ." He heard his own words come out too loud and scratchy, and he wished he could say what he really wanted to.

"You know, it's a pity your Texas rancher weren't grazing his cattle here in the Territory, as some ranchers do. Then you would always be here. I don't know the legalities involved, this being Indian land, but I understand some white cattlemen are doing well by pasturing their herds here."

"I know, Hannah, but my Texas rancher *ain't* here. Besides, since my back's been hurt, I don't know if . . . ."

"We all have to hope, about everything, Jess." Her voice was as soothing as the night breezes that brought him her fresh, sweet scent.

"Maybe so, but I wish things was different. I wish I hadn't made such a mess outta my life and . . . Well, I wish I'd met you a long time ago."

"If wishes were horses, beggars would ride." She smiled and stretched her legs and nudged off her sandals in a girlish movement to let her toes play in the dirt. The movement revealed her white feet and ankles and allowed her skirt to spread fan-like and settle against her legs to show, even in partial darkness, their lovely shape. Jess had never been so drawn to her.

"That's what my mother used to say," she said. "It's an old English proverb, published more than two-hundred years ago, I believe."

Jess found himself leaning closer to her. "Hannah, I'd sure like to come back, but you're ... You're the only lady I've ever known. And you know books and such, and I barely can read, and I'm ugly as a clod of dirt, and ... What I mean is, like they say, you can't make a silk purse out of a sow's ear."

She laughed – a pretty, musical sound. "I'm surprised you know that one. It's from an old English proverb, too – I believe it dates back to the early sixteen hundreds."

"Well, all I know is, it fits me. Me and you, Hannah, we're different, and . . . ."

"Jess!" She sounded almost scolding. "How are we so different? And what makes you think you're ugly? Some women like a man with rough but honest features, and with some gray in his mustache and sandy hair, and with sad brown eyes and a shy grin. It's like something I read just recently — and written by a woman, too, Margaret Wolfe Hungerford – 'Beauty is in the eye of the beholder.'"

Her voice was lower now, and more serious. "You're not a sow's ear, Jess. You're a good man, and I . . . ."

In the light of a partial moon, Jess saw she was even prettier than he thought – prettier than any woman he had ever seen. A strand of her clean-smelling hair stirred across her face in the breeze, and he thought he saw her green eyes turn moist.

Immediately, he was filled with the desire for a woman and the fondness for a true friend — and both of them were Hannah. He had never felt this way before and, if this turned out to be his last time to see her, he knew he would never feel this way again. His hand shot over to hers – and he felt himself go warm all over when she opened her hand to receive his. He squeezed her hand, and thought she lightly squeezed his in return, but wasn't sure.

Jess and Chago rode out of Darlington in the fresh daylight, with Jess standing in the stirrups and holding to the saddle horn to favor his sore back. They had said quick, formal good-byes to Hannah and Orna Mae outside the house. Jess suspected the boy felt the same way he did, as he had heard him sneak in shortly after he went to bed.

By sundown, they had made it to the road ranch known as Red Fork – and there two drifting cowboys who had ridden in from the north surprised them by telling about an attack by rustlers on Walker's trail herd. They had met the drive and stayed with the outfit overnight, swapping chores for meals, and saw it all. They said the rustlers were chased off, but did manage to drive off some of the saddle stock.

"I'd say they was lucky to get away from Big John Walker with their hides, let alone some horses," Jess said with a grin.

The next day they rode near the grave of Pat Hennessy, a freighter who was killed by Indians about six years before, Jess told Chago. He explained, though, that Indian trouble on the trail was rare anymore – that white outlaws were more common.

As it happened, a few minutes later Chago said, "Jess, we're about to meet two riders." He was standing in his stirrups and trying to better raise the figures on the horizon. "They look like Indians."

Jess unbuckled one of his saddlebags and took hold of his old Remington forty-four – but it soon appeared the two posed no threat. Both looked like Indians, with long hair and dark, blank faces, but one wore a white man's hat with rounded top and had a Mexican saddle on his iron-gray gelding. The other rode a scrawny yellowish mare. Both wore pistols and had rifles on their rigging.

After stopping for a brief conversation – much of it in sign language and very little in English – the two groups moved on.

"*Comancheros*, I'd call 'em," Jess said when they were out of earshot. "Glad they was friendly, but I wouldn't want to turn my back on 'em."

"Jess, I think they saw them rustlers we heard about," Chago said.

"What the heck you talkin' about? It didn't appear to me like they said anything about any horses."

"They said some things amongst themselves – some of it was in Spanish. One said he wondered if we was with the other *gringos* they saw a few days ago with the horses."

"I never could figure out how you can understand that Mexican, but you don't remember how to talk it," Jess said. "Well, horse traders go up and down this trail every so often."

"I guess you're right, Jess, but they said one of the horses was black with a white star between his eyes. And I remember a horse like that in the string – a good horse. If I didn't have Apple, I'd be proud to own 'im."

"Well, I doubt if we have to worry about them horse thieves. Big John Walker's probably puttin' salt on their tails right now."

Jess was glad he hadn't needed to bring his six-shooter into action. He had never wanted to use it for anything more than rattlesnakes and to scare coyotes away from baby calves.

In fact, hurting others in any way wasn't in his nature – although he had learned to be tough to survive. As a skinny, timid kid, he often took lickings from his foster brothers, until he became a dirty-fighting scrapper. He grinned to himself as he recalled the first time he got the best of one of his mean cousins.

They were weeding the cotton patch one hot Arkansas day when, during a quarrel over virtually nothing, the larger boy flattened him in the sand, and was coming at him again – until Jess grabbed his chopping hoe, jumped to one side, and whacked the boy so hard across the knees he heard the handle crack.

That night Jess and Chago camped in a cluster of cottonwoods not far from a small water hole. After eating some beef jerky and other grub, Jess lay in his blankets and closed his eyes, and soon was dreaming about Hannah.

It was nearly dawn when Jess was jarred awake by gunfire and excited yelling. Both he and Chago jumped up — to immediately duck back down, as shots popped and cracked and bullets whined. Jess spotted a rider as he passed in clear view in the dim light – he was on an iron-gray horse, and wore some of the garb of an Indian and a round-top hat.

"Them dang *Comancheros!*" Jess said, but in the same instant saw there were others – two white men, riding hard and firing behind the Indian-looking pair.

The two reined up. "Good morning, Mister Cravens. Looks like you're lucky we happened along just in time," one of them said. He was on a tall chestnut with a fancy California-style saddle, and was slender, maybe a little younger than Jess, and wore a spotted calfskin vest. Jess knew him – the one he had seen near the chuck wagon the day he got hurt in the stampede.

The other, Jess had never seen before. He was younger and, while round and shapeless, looked hard as granite and had a mean, ugly face – partly covered by his black mustache and beard.

"Actually," the first man said, smiling as he dismounted, "Coy here and I were chasing those Indians away from our camp, a short distance south of here – they were sneaking around, looking at our horses. We've been following you, and were going to catch up with you today anyway. We've got some business to talk over. Don't mind if we have some coffee, do you?"

Jess began stoking the fire to heat up the coffee, but didn't like the looks of their guests. He remembered more about the man, though he had known him on the trail drive only by sight and reputation. His name was Baggett – Emmit

Baggett. Other hands had said he was a smooth-talking drifter — lazy, and a crooked poker player.

Jess figured Walker must have told Baggett to take his bedding roll and drift, and that Baggett then picked up the mean-looking hombre someplace – the Territory was full of drifters and hard cases. But he couldn't imagine what they wanted from him.

Baggett grinned. "I thought you'd want to know, there's a federal reward poster in Caldwell with your picture on it — it's about that old stage holdup down in Texas."

He had known one of the men who was with Jess during the holdup, and heard all about it, and recognized Jess' name when he consigned his cattle at the Red River.

He grinned again, now looking like a gambler laying out a royal flush. "And you may not know this part: Remember that stage driver that got shot? Well, the poor man died."

Jess' heart pounded. Even though he hadn't done the shooting, he felt like a killer of an innocent man. And he could be jailed – maybe even hanged!

"Now, I don't want you to think we'd turn you in for the reward. But we do need a few thousand dollars, and that's what I estimate your cattle that are penned in Caldwell will bring. That, along with what we get for some horses we found running loose, will satisfy our needs quite well."

"Yeah, we heard about them horses. You have a lot of good luck, don't ya?" Jess said.

Baggett ignored the wry comment. "And since we're not going to say anything about your being the one on that wanted poster, I'm sure you won't mind returning the favor by signing this bill of sale that says those cows of yours belong to us." He pulled a folded paper out of his vest.

"We'll all go into Caldwell together, of course," he said, opening Jess' saddlebags and finding the pistol, which he handed to his partner, whom he also addressed as Sanderson. "And as soon as we collect the money for the herd, you and the young man here will be free to head back to Texas."

Jess wondered if he had much choice. Baggett could be bluffing, but the one called Coy Sanderson stood nearby, his thick arms folded and looking like he would do anything Baggett told him. He wore a gun of his own, plus Jess' pistol in his belt.

"Well, we might as well have some coffee while I think this over," Jess said, figuring on stalling for time. The big coffeepot was now making a boiling sound.

"Jess! Jess! Apple's been shot!" Chago was yelling from where their horses were picketed.

Jess ran to the boy. The little horse stood, in an awkward, spraddle-legged position, his head down, and made deep, groaning sounds as he breathed in and out. The early sun glistened on something moist at the pony's middle. Jess put his hand there and felt the warm, sticky liquid.

"He caught a bullet, Jess! I shoulda come out to see about 'im right after all that shootin'."

"It wouldn't have made any difference, boy. You couldn't help it." It was all Jess knew to say. He dreaded looking at Chago.

Sanderson stalked over, pulled out his pistol and directed it at the pony's head. "A hoss with a bullet in it ain't much good," he said, and fired.

Chago couldn't have looked much worse if the bullet had hit him.

Coy looked at Chago and grinned, and stomped back toward the fire.

Jess checked himself from tearing into Coy with both fists. Not only was he a mountain of a man, but both he and Baggett were armed, and held the upper hand.

Baggett and his partner moved into camp, picketing the six stolen horses nearby, and soon were sitting around the fire drinking coffee, lacing it occasionally with whiskey.

Jess noticed Chago staring at the two. The boy's mouth was closed tightly, his jaw muscles flexing, and the look in his large eyes was something Jess had never seen before – like the kid was about to do something crazy.

Chago, still with the fierce stare, walked straight toward the two men, picked up the dirty bandanna used to handle the coffeepot and took hold of the handle as if to pour – and swung the hot, nearly full pot smack against Coy Sanderson's head. The steaming liquid splashed all over the man's upper body as he fell to his knees, screaming cusswords.

But Sanderson rose quickly and threw one hand over the side of his face and grabbed for Chago with the other.

"Chago, get away from 'im!" Jess yelled as the boy, who already had clawed in vain for Jess' pistol in the man's belt, ducked the grab, and ran and snatched up the reins of Baggett's grazing horse and leaped into the saddle.

But Sanderson, amazingly fast, had headed for the horse in the same instant and with his left hand caught the reins and with his right fist made a looping swing that knocked Chago off the horse.

Jess started forward, but got only a few feet before Baggett had the muzzle of a Winchester under his chin, and clicked the hammer back.

Sanderson, his mean eyes wide and his face now a terrible grin, jerked the dazed Chago to his feet. "I guess you know what's in store for you, you skinny little greaser – you was stealin' a hoss!" The big man grabbed his lariat off his saddle and shook out a loop. His eyes were glowing with feverish anger and an evil anticipation.

Jess felt the most terrible dread of his life shudder through his body, and he tried again to move from under Baggett's rifle. "Now listen here, you . . . ."

But to Jess' surprise, Baggett himself broke in. "Ah, come on, Coy, don't get that upset. You do something like that and we'll have trouble with the law for sure." He moved over and laid a hand, brotherly like, on his partner's shoulder.

But Sanderson shoved Baggett away, whipped out his pistol and waved it at both men. He pulled a leather string from his pocket and tied Chago's hands behind him, then seized Chago by the belt and swung him, like a rag doll, up onto Baggett's chestnut.

"You wanted to ride that hoss – now you're gonna ride 'im. You're gonna look up a limb, boy!" he said as he tossed the loop over Chago's head and yanked it tight while pulling the horse under a thick branch and throwing the other end of the rope over it.

Jess saw the boy's big eyes go moist with fear, and sweat shine on his olive face and neck – which already swelled above where the rope grew tighter. It all was happening so quickly that Jess, nearly paralyzed with horror, almost couldn't believe the nightmare taking place before him.

Chago's eyes bulged and his face turned a purple that Jess had never seen. The boy made a gagging sound. Sanderson, his pistol now holstered, flipped the free end of the rope behind him like a whip.

As he lashed at the horse's rump, Jess made his move. He shoved past Baggett and dove headfirst into Sanderson, thinking only of overcoming his foe before being either shot down or struck dead. He had to give Chago one precious instant to free himself.

Jess hoped to snatch the rope from Sanderson with one hand and grab at the man's most tender parts with the other, while thrusting his head under his bearded chin and sinking his teeth into the massive, dirty throat. But instead, he crashed his body into Sanderson's, butting his head into the man's face. A thundering blow landed on the side of his head, and his body went limp.

Seconds later, Jess rose on one elbow to look through a blur at Sanderson, still holding the rope – but, curiously, no longer taut – and Chago, still attached to the other end of it.

Jess remembered only his struggling with the big man, the horse rearing, and Chago tumbling off, right on top of both him and Sanderson. And the rope, somehow – maybe he *had* managed to grab it from Sanderson after all – had gone slack just in time to save Chago from a choking death or broken neck.

Jess was thanking his luck when he heard Chago's voice,

and saw him looking as if he saw something to the north. "Hey, somebody's comin'."

Jess at first thought the boy was trying to trick their two captors, but turned and saw the cloud of dust. One of the stolen horses whickered. Jess was instantly buoyed. No matter who it was, it meant hope for him and Chago.

The faraway figures grew clearer — dark forms of cattle and a few taller outlines of horses and riders under the rising dust.

Baggett turned to his partner. "It looks like a small herd, Coy, moving east from the main trail. We'd best get moving and appear like everything's normal."

Sanderson grumbled, but started for his horse.

Drovers often drifted their herds off the trail to fatten them on the lush grass here and farther north in the Cherokee Outlet – also called "the Strip." And passing more herds, and more people, should mean safety for Jess and Chago, at least until they reached Caldwell.

When they pulled out, Jess and Chago, their hands tied in front, rode double on Grasshopper, behind the herd of stolen horses and in front of their two captors. They would be shot, they were told, if they signaled in any way as they passed the drovers.

Jess felt better than he had in several days, and didn't know why, as they weren't out of danger by a long shot.

"You all right, Chago?" he said.

"Yeah, I guess so, Jess. You?"

"Yeah. In fact, I feel better than I ought to, considerin'," Jess said. "My back is still sore; my head feels like it's been kicked by a mule; I'm dirty and itchy all over; I gotta taste in my mouth like I been eatin' green persimmons; and I might be in jail, or dead, in a day or two – but for some reason, I feel right pert."

About dark they stopped on a rise covered with scraggly blackjack trees a short piece from a sinkhole. The outlaws picketed the stolen horses near the water, and the other horses nearer the camp, as they normally did to be ready in case of trouble.

Jess spent a comfortable enough evening in camp – even with their hands tied, he and Chago managed to eat their meager servings and take care of themselves – and Jess still felt good as he crawled into his bedding.

But he wished he could somehow make Chago feel better. The boy needed some cheering up. It was plain he was still feeling low about Apple. Also, he was staring straight ahead and flexing his jaw muscles – like he did before he flew into Coy with the hot coffeepot.

Jess, not wanting him to try something like that again, planned to stay awake for a while and keep an eye on the boy.

But he didn't. As soon as he stretched out, he fell asleep – and into the most beautiful dream he had ever had.

Hannah was holding out both hands to him and smiling, and she was more beautiful than he had ever seen her. They moved closer, and the first touch of her fingers gave him rivulets of excitement. And just as suddenly all his shyness, all his indecision, all the obstacles – his cattle, his obligation to Mr. McKenzie, his feelings of both resentment and guilt about Chago – were gone. And he took her in his arms, pulling her against him with loving gentleness, and a youthfulness and strength he hadn't felt in years.

And later, as the breeze still stirred the thin window curtains, she lay in his arms as they talked, about nothing – until, with no words between them, they belonged to each other.

When Jess woke, he tried to keep her image from leaving like a wisp of fog in the growing daylight. But he knew he would always remember the dream as actual experience – his love for her would last forever. And he knew that nothing else in his life was important to him.

Jess heard an excited yell, then more yells mixed with cusswords. He sat up and turned to Chago – or where Chago should have been.

"The little greaser's gone!" It was Sanderson's angry bellow. "And he took the hoss herd with 'im – all six of 'em!"

Baggett was already saddling his chestnut. "I'll stop him! All I've gotta do is get close enough for a shot – either at him or the horse he's on." He jammed his Winchester into its holster.

Jess was stunned. It didn't make sense, why Chago would run off, without telling him — and take all the stolen horses.

That was it! The boy had made a run for help, and slipped off without him because he could move quieter, and faster, alone. And he had taken the six horses so he could hop from one to another when they began to tire. Chago could do that, even if his hands were still tied.

Baggett told Sanderson to follow, bringing Jess. "When I get the boy, I'll wait up ahead. And I'll get him."

He spurred off in a gallop, following the horse tracks that led northward.

Sanderson on his horse, followed by Jess on Grasshopper and the packhorse farther back, were going at a steady jog about noon when they came upon a grazing horse — a medium-sized gelding, its bay coat still streaked with white lines of dried sweat.

Sanderson glared at Jess. "That's one of the hoss herd – why'd that crazy kid turn it loose?" The big man wasn't quick at figuring things out.

Jess shrugged. "I got no idy."

Sanderson grunted and jabbed his horse with his spurs, and they moved out in a lope.   About two hours later they passed another loose horse, a tired-looking roan mare. Sanderson grunted again and spurred his horse, already in a good sweat, back into a lope.   They soon came to another jaded pony, a stout paint gelding, but this time Sanderson didn't slow down or make a sound.

They stopped about sundown where a clearing had been chopped out in a small grove of locust trees a year or so before – apparently by drovers who made camp there, near a stream called the Salt Fork.

Jess was glad for the chance to rest, but could tell Sanderson was in one of his meanest moods.

"You put 'im up to this, didn't ya?" he said, staring at Jess over the campfire after making coffee to go with some beef jerky and cold biscuits. He also had been sloshing whiskey into his cup, and his eyes had an especially dangerous glint in the flickering firelight.

Jess didn't answer. He figured he and the big man would lock horns sooner or later, but with hands tied and in his weakened condition, now wasn't the time. He braced himself for what was coming.

Sanderson got up and walked around the fire to stand over Jess. "You hear me? Did you put that boy up to runnin' off with them hosses?"

Jess didn't remember much after the first kick – barely feeling the powerful blow to the side of his sore head, and a half dozen savage kicks to his side. He sank into a sick state of half-sleep that surely was death. But the pain and his own groans kept telling him he was still alive.

Jess woke in the cool freshness just before dawn, and lay thinking, and wondering, despite his misery. Chago could be safely in Kansas by now – or shot by Baggett, or in jail in Caldwell as an accused horse thief. And he himself could soon be in jail for the old stagecoach robbery and shooting.

It could be, Jess thought, that his past was about to catch up with him and claim his life – along with the life of the poor kid he took, reluctantly, to raise.

Good things had happened, too, since he and the boy had left Texas with the small herd of cattle. He had met Hannah, of course, and Chago had changed – or maybe his feelings about the boy had changed; he wasn't sure.

If he could only find out about Chago. If he could somehow get out of his present mess, but getting away from the insane giant that held him captive seemed hopeless.

Night was shifting into day as the vague forms of tree-

---

tops, bushes and the items around the dying coals of the fire began taking shape, and in seconds the sun broke across the top of the eastern horizon — but made a ghostly light in a heavy fog that had settled in.

Sanderson was now up, stoking the fire, and Jess knew he would soon yell at him to go tend to the horses. Jess watched the huge man move about as he fixed a hurried breakfast of sorts and got his gear together, his spurs making a soft jingle as his large boots stomped across the grassy earth – the same boots that had nearly kicked Jess to death.

Not that such beatings were new to him, having grown up the way he had, and he recalled again his last licking before he left home – the time in the cotton patch before he grabbed the chopping hoe and . . . .

A chopping hoe!

That was it! There *was* a chance. Even with his hands tied in front, he could still swing a pole of some kind – if he could find one, and if he could catch Sanderson unawares long enough to use it, and if he even had the strength.

Sanderson shouted at him to bring in the horses – and the thundering voice reminded him that if he failed, this could be his last act of any kind.

Jess pulled himself up and moved toward the horses, his eyes sweeping over the wet ground among the trees – and seeing nothing more than a twig or two.

Sanderson hiked something out of his throat and spat, and growled for him to hurry.

Jess mumbled an acknowledgement as he reached the place where the horses were picketed and now stood, like dozing statues, in the small area they had grazed and trampled.

He kept looking frantically around him, and spotted it – part of an old wagon tongue, barely visible where briar bushes had grown around it, and with one end blackened. It could have been left by an outfit that grazed a herd here; maybe a cracked tongue had been replaced, and one end of it fed into a campfire.

It was much shorter than its original length, but appeared light enough to be handled, though still plenty heavy – not as easily swung as a chopping hoe, but surely capable of doing more damage.

And that was what Jess was going to do with it.

He led Sanderson's horse away from the others and past several small trees and bushes, and dropped the rope, leaving the animal to graze. As quietly as possible, he pulled the piece of wood from the brush, and crouched behind the briar cover, the cloud of fog helping to hide him.

His heart pounding, Jess waited to hear the big man's booming voice again.

"What's takin' ya so long with them hosses?"

Jess tightened his grip on his crude weapon. "Something's wrong with your horse, Sanderson. He's actin' funny."

"What the . . . ." Right away the man came lumbering toward Jess' position of ambush.

Jess drew in a deep breath and held it until Sanderson was just past the briar bushes and, to the best of his judgement, about half a wagon tongue away.

"Right here!" he yelled, and swung the heavy piece of timber, at knee level, thrusting every fiber of muscle and bit of will he had into it.

It was shortly before sundown when Jess, with Pal at the end of a long rope, and carrying Sanderson, now disarmed and his hands tied behind him and tied to the packhorse, saw the line of trees up ahead that was the Salt Fork of the Arkansas River. He knew Caldwell was just on the other side.

He immediately felt relief – but worry, too. They had passed two more worn-out horses, which probably meant Chago was riding the last one. But there was no way to know what had happened, or was about to happen.

He drew closer, and spotted two riders on the far bank of the river, their horses standing. The smaller rider was sitting bareback on a black horse, and looked like . . . .

"Chago!" Jess heard himself yell it out.

Right away he recognized the other rider, a large man sitting straight in the saddle on what looked like a stout buckskin. It was Big John Walker.

After Jess forded the river, he saw Chago was grinning – obviously at seeing Sanderson tied and roughed-up. Jess figured the look on the kid's face was worth all his sore spots.

"Howdy, Cravens," Walker said, and he was grinning, too, at the sight of Sanderson. "I don't know how you managed to bring that big buffalo in like a calf tied for the brandin' fire, especially since not long ago you couldn't hardly climb out of a chuck wagon – but I'll take 'im off your hands now."

But Walker shifted in the saddle and looked like he dreaded what he was going to say next. "I got a lot to tell ya, Cravens. His partner is in the calaboose already — Baggett. But I didn't get 'im soon enough. He slipped into town before I knowed it, and forged a bill of sale and stole your cattle. And before I caught up to 'im, he'd already lost the money gamblin' in Wichita."

The trail boss said that after he got the herd to Caldwell, he started back into the Territory to look for the six stolen horses and the horse thieves – but met Chago, who had just made it into Kansas.

While Chago was explaining everything to him, and while he was getting a warrant for the arrests of both Baggett and Sanderson, Baggett slipped in and stole Jess' cattle.

Walker glanced at Sanderson. "As to this big buffalo . . . Well, I'll tell ya about him later – first I wanna talk about you." His eyes narrowed and glinted with amusement. "You came near gettin' in a little trouble yourself, didn't ya?"

Jess heard himself stammer, as Walker went on. "And you can thank your boy here for doin' his best to get you out of it. Not only did he ride like the devil to get here, aimin' to save you from the horse thieves, but then he tried to hide your criminal background – even if he had a funny way of goin' about it."

Chago had tried to find wanted posters on Jess, so he could swipe them before any of the local lawmen paid any serious attention to it, Walker explained.

"The fact is, there *ain't* a wanted poster on you any-where – not anymore. Texas lawmen have a lot more to worry about than a two-bit little holdup by three bumblin' saddle tramps. Besides, Baggett lied to you about a murder charge. The stage driver was shot in the right foot, and he walked kinda peculiar for a while, but he died of old age about a year ago."

He paused, glancing at Chago, then back at Jess. "I'll tell ya somethin' — poster or not, if I was you I'd be glad I had a son like him, who would try to do so much for me. He *is* your son, ain't he? As I recall, you never mentioned it, but that's what *he* told me."

As for Baggett, Walker said, "I knowed he was the cheeky type when I hired him on, but I needed hands. I'll be more careful in the future."

"Oh, and about his big buffalo . . ." His eyes took on some playfulness. "Cravens, after all that's happened to you, you did have one little piece of luck: There's a RE-ward out for Sanderson – however, it ain't as big as it oughta be. When it was first posted, I guess it wasn't known just how bad he really was. Turns out he's wanted for killin' at least one man he stole some cattle from."

Walker shifted in the saddle again. "As to the RE-ward you're gonna get, I already penciled it down on paper – I figured you wouldn't mind – and I can tell ya what it comes to. Figurin' what beef is sellin' for, the RE-ward money is worth right at half the herd you lost – twenty head."

"So, that means you're only half as bad off as you thought you was. Or, figurin' another way – since, as you mentioned, half that forty head you consigned to my outfit belonged to your boss – you might say that on this whole drive, you broke even."

Walker, who because of his ties with the stock raisers association knew about such things, then gave him some advice that was something like closing the barn door after the horse was stolen. He suggested that Jess register his brand, like many cattlemen were doing now – "in case you ever get back in the business and have some more cows."

"If your brand had been registered," Walker said, "you just might not have lost everything the way you did, since that makes thieves more careful about who they steal from."

"However," Walker said, "you *did* come out a smidgen ahead on this trip. For one thing, you and your boy helped me catch these horse thieves and find them stolen horses. For another . . . Well, I feel kinda bad about puttin' you off at Darlington, since that's what led to you losin' your cattle. So, I'm payin' ya both full wages – in fact, top-hand wages – just like you had been on the drive all the way: a hundred dollars for ya both. I figure that's fair."

"Not only that," he said, "but since this young fella fancies this black horse, I'm givin' it to 'im. I figure with that race he made gettin' here, he earned it."

He added: "And I even talked the marshal into givin' the boy Baggett's fancy saddle, instead of auctionin' it off along with his mount like he was plannin' to do. Baggett won't be needin' either one for quite a spell."

Jess couldn't remember ever feeling better as he and Chago got up after a long night's sleep in their hotel room. They had each taken a warm, leisurely bath the evening before, then gone into a nearby café and filled themselves with a supper of steak and potatoes. And now they were washing up for a big breakfast.

Not only could Jess pay Mr. McKenzie for his twenty head of cattle with the reward money, but Chago had a good horse to replace Apple, and they both had enough money to get all three horses re-shod, buy some supplies, get a haircut and a new shirt apiece, and even have a little left over.

And now Jess thought he knew why he was feeling so good earlier on the trail – and he couldn't imagine wanting Chago to go on his own hook. It all had something to do with the Bible story the boy hold him in Darlington; and the way Jess felt about Hannah – which somehow changed the way he felt about life in general.

Besides, he was looking forward to Chago's help in starting a new herd when they got back to Texas.

Jess even thought about taking in one of Caldwell's better saloons after sundown – there *were* a few places tamer than the Red Light, a combination saloon, dance hall and whorehouse with a vile reputation. He would drink a glass or two of beer, play some billiards and a hand of cards, and laugh a little with the sporting girls.

But now that things had changed between them, and he thought of the boy as more like a partner, he wouldn't feel right about leaving him alone while he enjoyed himself. Maybe they could do it together next time they came to Caldwell, when the boy would be older – providing, that is, they ever had another herd to take up the trail.

Anyway, Jess felt sure they both were thinking more about heading back to Darlington for a few days, and planning for what promised to be a happy future.

But then Chago told him he was going on his own hook.

The boy said he had met a family in town who were headed for Texas, and had asked him to go along. He had agreed to go part of the way – as far as Darlington, where he would stay, and marry Orna Mae.

"Dang it!" Jess said. "I knew when you got thicker than molasses with that little gal it was gonna cause me trouble sooner or later. I ain't sayin' you shouldn't get married if you want to – even if you *are* too young and wet behind the ears – but you got a place to live with me at the ranch in Texas."

"Not only that," he added, "but I still owe ya somethin', and since I don't have the cattle money, I'll have to help you in some other way, whether you get married or not. And if you don't go back with me, I never will feel right about it!"

"That's all right, Jess. You don't owe me nothin'." Chago's voice was mild as usual, but it had a firmness about it. "And I've got a good horse and saddle, and when I get there I'm gonna work for that blacksmith. He told me he needed the help."

The family would leave in about a week, Chago said – a few days after he and Jess had first planned to pull out.

Things never happened the way they should, Jess was thinking later that morning as he walked toward the livery barn, carrying his few belongings after checking out of the hotel. Now that he was going by himself, he would pull out a few days earlier than he had planned, and be at Darlington before Chago's arrival, as further words between them would only make the situation more awkward.

Chago met him in front of the livery. He boy must have come to tell him good-bye. "I guess . . . I guess you're pullin' out today, ain't you, Jess?"

"Yeah, pretty soon. You'll be leavin' a few days later with the folks that have the wagon, that right?" Jess hoped his voice sounded normal, but didn't think it did.

Chago swallowed before speaking. "Jess, I don't want ya to feel bad or nothin' because I'm not goin' with ya, and ... ."

He looked down, and with the toe of his boot scraped some dirt off the boardwalk. "And I want ya to know it don't matter about what Mister Walker said, about me bein' your son – I just told him that because it was easier to explain that way, and . . . Well, people just don't understand about me and you."

"I know, Chago. And you oughta be able to go on your own hook if that's what you want. But I want ya to know, if ya ever need my help . . . ." Jess had trouble saying more, and looked down and found his own dirt to move around with his toe.

After a moment, he didn't know what else to do, so in a quick, jerky motion stuck out his hand. And as he did he realized – and suspected Chago did also – that it was their first handshake.

If ya ever need my help . . . . What a fool thing to say, Jess thought. Even if the boy ever did need his help, he had none to give.

The worst of it was, because of the way things had happened, he would spend the rest of his days knowing he still owed the boy – only a heap more than the earnings from twenty cows.

That made Jess think of something else he should do before leaving – stop by and say farewell to Big John Walker, who probably would be at the shipping yard, looking at cattle.

Jess headed that way, and walked by the office where cattlemen could register their brands, and thought idly about Walker's advice – which Jess wished he had heard earlier. Maybe no one would have tried to steal his cattle in the first place if his and Chago's brand had been registered. Maybe ... .

His and Chago's brand!

That was it – there was something he could give the boy after all!

It wasn't much – didn't amount to anything, in fact, and it was even kind of a joke. But it meant something to him, and he knew it was the right thing to do. He wheeled and yelled at Chago.

A few minutes later, the man behind the desk, looking expectantly at Jess, then at Chago – who was still puzzled – asked, "What's the name and what brand?"

Jess first glanced sideways at Chago, whose expression said it was just dawning on him what was going on, then grinned and blurted it out: "Jess Cravens and son, Santiago Cravens. Let's make it the *Double C!*"

Neither one of them felt like they had to say anything as they walked back, with Jess feeling good – despite all his hard luck, he had at least figured out a way to tell Chago something he felt he had to tell him.

At the door of the livery, they shook hands again, and Jess grinned and said, "When you start blacksmithin', I want ya to hammer out that *Double C* brand – even if it's just for passin' on to my foster grandkids. You can tell 'em that's the nearest I got to payin' what I owe ya."

For the first time, Chago gave him a hard look and

raised his voice. "You know what, I'm gettin' tired of hearin' you say that!"

Jess frowned. The boy was as sassy as ever.

Chago shook his finger in Jess' face. "You don't owe me nothin'. You took me with you when you didn't have to, and you done the best you could for me ever since. And that was enough. You never could understand, Jess. I don't want somethin' because you think you *owe* it to me. Now if you *want* to give me something, well, that's different. Like puttin' my name on that brand – that was one of the few things you ever gave me because you *wanted to*. And I'm prouder of that than I would be of a whole bunch of cows."

Jess tried to say something, but Chago cut him off. "That's the reason I'm goin' on my own hook, Jess – because you keep talkin' about how you owed me half of that cattle money that we lost. Now, if you was to ask me to go back and help you at the ranch because you *want* me to, well, I'd be proud to."

"Whoa now, I thought you was goin' back to that little gal. I thought . . . ."

"I am, Jess. I'm gonna marry Orna Mae, but we'll live on the ranch, not in Darlington – that is, if you *want* is to. We'll have to build a house, though – she already said that little sod hut won't do for all of us."

Jess thought for a long moment before saying anything. When he did, he had to swallow first. "Well, I'd sure be obliged if you'd come home with me, because . . . Well, it's because . . . ."

"That's all right, Jess. You don't have to tell me things over and over, like you always do."

Soon, both were talking excitedly about their plans – first, spending a few days at Darlington, then going back to Jess' job at the Texas ranch and start building a new herd. Maybe, Jess said, they could get Mr. McKenzie to expand his herd, and acquire some of the grazing land in the Territory – and Chago liked that idea, too.

"But you know what, Jess? I'm proud to be goin' back

to the ranch and all, but it's too bad we're gonna have to wait so long to have even one head to put our brand on. Figurin' that way, we made this whole trip for nothin'."

Jess looked up sharply, and now it was his time to be indignant. "Whoa now! What ya mean, this trip was for nothin'? It for dang sure wasn't for nothin' for me, and it's not just because of who we got to know at Darlington, either. This drive taught me things I never would have figured out by myself."

"But I'm like you, boy," he added, "I can hardly wait till we get our very first steer to put that new brand on."

Someone yelled. "Cravens! I gotta talk to ya about somethin'." Jess turned and saw Big John Walker coming horseback from the direction of the cattle pens.

"Well, wonder what's wrong now!" he said to Chago. "I thought our luck was runnin' too good."

Walker lowered his voice as he got closer. "The boys got a stray runnin' loose. They say it's got my road brand on it, and another brand they couldn't make out at a distance, but it sounded to me like it's one of yours. Could be when Baggett stole your herd, he missed one."

Jess was relieved. At least, it wasn't bad news. "Well now, looks like we'll have something to put our new brand on even before we leave for home!" he said to Chago. "We'll drive it back to Texas – it'll be the first of our new herd."

Walker was still talking. "The way it appears, it busted outta the pen before the rest of your cattle got moved out. And it's been causin' trouble all over town."

Trouble?

Jess glanced at Chago, who was looking back with a similar expression. And they both knew what Walker would say next: "It's that ornery steer of yours with a crooked horn."

Jess' and Chago's eyes locked, and despite all he could do to keep serious, Jess felt his face crack into a grin, and Chago's did the same.

Walker was grinning, too, and went on. "They said yesterday evenin' it was cavortin' around over on the east side

---

of town – said it even had the ladies at the Red Light scared to go to the little house out back."

In seconds Jess and Chago were bent over with laughter. Jess hurt in his back, but his moans gave way to more explosions of mirth that he couldn't control, and he didn't care.

"Just before dark they lost it in the woods around Big Casino Creek," Walker said. "They found it early this mornin', headin' south toward the river. They're bringin' it back to the pens now – tryin' to, anyhow. One of the boys said it's harder to herd than a wild hog."

Jess managed to say something to Chago between gags, coughs and hoots. "I'll tell ya one thing, it won't be hard to drive *that* devilish ol' critter back to Texas. The only thing, we might wear the horses out tryin' to keep up with 'im."

And as they looked at each other through tears of laughter, Jess realized – and he knew that Chago did, too – that it was their first time to laugh together.

A little later they were saddling their mounts and rigging the packhorse for the trip south. They would get as far as they could before dark, then break camp early and be back on the trail before daylight tomorrow. They had a long way to go, special people to see at Darlington, then important things to do back in Texas.

For the first time in Jess' life, he felt like celebrating.

He stopped just as he was about to pull the cinch on Grasshopper, and turned to Chago. "Whoa now! I just remembered somethin'. We can't go yet. We gotta check back into the hotel for one more night and get washed up!"

Chago looked startled.

Jess looked back at him with as serious an expression as he could muster. "There's one more reason this drive wasn't for nothin'! You said somethin' about wantin' to raise a little hades in Caldwell. Didn't ya?"

The following is an imaginative description of "the Cook Gang" of outlaws, along with a remote store operated by Xerxes "Zack" Taylor, during the 1890s in the Cherokee Nation of Indian Territory, near present-day Tahlequah and Hulbert. It's also colored by one of the author's boyhood memories.

The Last Holdup

Matt Coulter rode out with his four partners in the early darkness, their mounts moving head to tail through the woods. The only sounds were the soft, rhythmic clop of the horses and the squeak of saddle leather, until came the far-away *yip-yip-yip* of coyotes. Matt liked the lonesome, wild, free call. It was times like this that he wished he could go back a ways and change his grown-up life.

He would feel better, of course, if he'd had his coffee — it had been a dry camp, and he sorely missed it. Normally, it was his favorite time, when the smell of the Arbuckle's boiling over the crackles of burning sticks in the air's freshness was something close to Heaven. He loved sipping a cup while watching and hearing the new day wake up.

Presently, the riders came out onto an opening that glowed white under a descending moon. Matt heard a horse snort, and turned to see McKee ride up beside him.

"If ya ask me, this ain't gonna be worth the trouble," McKee said. "I doubt if old man Walters has ever had as much as twenty dollars in his whole store. Seems loco to me. But maybe Del knows what he's doin'."

Matt didn't reply. His first holdup some years back hadn't made much sense, either. He and another young cowhand decided to rob a rancher they had worked for down in the Choctaw Nation. He had dismissed them, and still owed them some wages. Cowboy work had started slacking off in Indian Territory, with times getting hard — though Matt, for one, fancied himself handy with his pistol and welcomed the situation as a chance to show off.

But it went bad. The rancher put up a fight, and there was shooting. No one was hurt, but they had to ride hard back to the Cherokee Nation and lay low.

Matt had been laying low ever since, when not stealing or robbing. Now, like the men he rode with, he was wanted, and he lived by his gun because he had to.

McKee, who had still been murmuring, was cut off by Delford Combs, who was riding up front. "Shut up! I said for everybody to keep quiet. And if I was you, McKee, I'd remember who's boss!"

Combs, whose voice carried authority even in hushed tones, was the leader because he was quick with his gun and had a dangerous temper. The others, including Matt, found it easier to take orders from him than argue.

Combs had laid out the plans the night before: They were getting too well-known in the Indian country, so would pull out west for Oklahoma Territory and hold up a train depot Combs knew about, then maybe head down to Texas or out to New Mexico Territory. But first they would rob Zeke Walters' little store. They needed whatever they might get.

Matt barely knew Walters, who was bony and stooped and looked like most old men. But he understood why Combs had targeted the store, even if the take would be small.

It was close to where they had been hiding out. Also, it was on a trail that crossed Fourteen Mile Creek, which because of heavy spring rains was now running high, and they weren't likely to encounter other travelers there, especially before daylight.

Also, only old Zeke and his wife lived there, in the back

　　　　　　　　　　　　　　Thunder in the Heartland

of the small building. They didn't even have a dog.

Moreover, they hadn't pulled any holdups for a while, and Matt knew idleness made Combs even more touchy than normal. The man was itching for action.

But Matt hadn't liked the Oklahoma Territory idea. He hadn't said so in camp, but now decided to speak up. "Del, I know you're boss, but I hear that federal marshal over at Guthrie has been throwin' a pretty wide loop, especially after that shoot-out in Ingalls. Maybe we oughta . . . ."

Combs jerked his horse to a stop and wheeled in the saddle, his right hand at his holster. "You wanna dispute me, do ya, Coulter? We got business to take care of, but I'd just as soon put this job off and slap leather with you right here and now."

It was dark, but Matt could feel the violence in the man's gaze. He opened his mouth to reply, but looked away instead and swallowed a gob of pride.

Ever since he met Combs, he had truly wondered, should they ever come to a fight, if he could stand up against the man — and he hoped he would never find out. If he lost, a few bitter words just weren't a good reason to die.

Since taking up the outlaw trail, Matt had come to know more than he wanted about dying — and killing.

Once when they robbed a post office at Fort Gibson, the clerk handed over the money — but not quick enough to suit Combs. He'd shot the little man in the face.

But Combs, while far meaner than most, wasn't the only bandit who killed.

Matt had soon learned there was more to being on the scout than being quick at getting a Colt in your hand and shooting tomato cans off a rock. When you lived by the gun, you killed with it.

There was that fateful day when they were stealing a settler's horses and the man ran out and threw down on them with a Winchester. Matt, startled, drew and fired — and instantly wished he hadn't. His forty-four slug had found its mark.

He seldom closed his eyes at night without seeing what

---

he had done. And Matt knew that, sooner or later, something like that would happen again — if, that is, he himself survived that long.

That was something else he knew, even if his partners didn't. The days of the outlaw, like those of the cowboy, were nearing an end. More settlers were coming, along with fences, and more lawmen, too.

Outlaws, like never before, were on the run — like coyotes being chased across land that once was free and open but now was being sectioned off and turned by the plow.

All of that had dawned on him too late, and now Matt wasn't sure which he feared more — his own death, either on the gallows or by a bullet from a deputy, or someone like Combs. Or having to kill another innocent man.

Unless, of course, he broke away from men of his kind and changed his ways, finding honest work, and a decent life – but that was just more of his wistful thinking before full light of day.

Still, maybe that was the only trail left for him — narrow though it was.

While he couldn't change the past, he might hide from it — go far away, change his life completely, even if it meant hard, humble labor such as cleaning stables or swamping saloons and dance halls.

It would mean either standing up to Combs, or running.

But maybe he *could* break away, when the time was right. Maybe even after this next holdup. Maybe . . . .

The riders pulled up at the creek where it churned the crossing into a deep, muddy swirl and washed on through the cottonwoods and sycamores. They would wait here for daylight. Walters' store wasn't far away.

Soon, the darkness gave way to a pale light, and a little beyond the creek and up in a clearing were the soft outlines of the little store and few outbuildings. A rooster crowed. There was only a short time to wait. Matt shifted in the saddle.

It was on such a morning many years ago in Arkansas, Matt recalled, that he first went fishing — the memory, for the very first time, flashing before him as clear as the coming day. Maybe it was the same certain instant of twilight, the same freshness of the clean, new morning and the damp, rich greenness, the same sound of moving, gurgling water.

He was a small boy, and the old gent who helped his father by repairing harness and doing light farm work — a "Mr. Whittington" — knew how badly Matt wanted to go, so promised to take him, if it didn't rain.

Matt prayed it wouldn't, and woke at dawn, his heart racing. He ran to the window and held out his hand, and the few sprinkles on his palm along with the thick darkness overhead nearly put him in tears.

But soon the skies cleared just enough for Mr. Whittington to approve the trip, and Matt was lifted by a joy the likes of which he had never known.

"Well, got your pole and line ready, Matthew?" Matt recalled the man's amused smile.

For the first time, it came to Matt that the old gent really hadn't wanted to go — that the long walk on a day that turned hot and muggy was hard on him.

Matt had long forgotten the happiness he felt, skipping barefoot ahead of Mr. Whittington down the path toward the river. And what a pity that the old gent never knew the little thing he did for a boy would someday be a man's most priceless memory — and the only genuinely valuable possession of a worldly outlaw!

Mr. Whittington now would be long dead, and Matt so wished that several years ago he had gone back to where he grew up, just to thank the old man for that small act of kindness.

At one time he would have laughed at such a thought, but now his regret was an actual pain — the hopeless wish that he could say something nice to someone who was no longer within earshot.

They crossed the creek, the rush of water loud against

their stirrups. Up the rise, the store was now a solid object in the realness of the new day, the yellow glow in a window from an inside lamp giving in to the greater natural brightness.

Zeke Walters would be slowly moving around. Matt pictured the old man. He'd be glad when this robbery was over and done.

Combs reined up. "Coulter, since you and McKee don't like the way I'm runnin' things, you must be itchin' to do somethin' — so you two ride on up. We'll keep watch down here. And remember, keep it quiet if you can, because I wanna get outta this country without runnin' from a posse. But don't take no fuss — no matter what ya have to do, get the money! Ya understand, Coulter?"

Matt heard himself speak up. "Del, I'm not tryin' to dispute ya, but why don't we just forget this job? Like McKee says, Zeke Walters likely ain't got much money anyhow. We could ride on and . . . ."

Combs stiffened, and Matt could see his eyes flash with anger even in the faint light. "Well now, Coulter, maybe I *will* forget this job – that is, until I teach you who's boss once and for all." His voice was loud. He swung down from the saddle.

McKee and the others were still.

Matt knew he had made an irreversible mistake, but tried anyway to soothe matters. "Del, I didn't mean to argue with ya. I was just sayin' that . . . ."

"Shut up and get off your horse!" Combs' voice was even, his manner calm, his eyes unblinking like those of a rattlesnake. His gun hand was cupped, inches from his holster.

Matt didn't move. "Del, I'm not lookin' to fight with ya." Talk, Matt figured, was still his best option.

"Whichever way you want it, Coulter — on your horse or on the ground. Whenever you're ready, go for that iron!"

Again, Matt didn't move. He was making a wise decision — though he wasn't sure if he could move if he wanted to; his whole body seemed paralyzed; his right arm hung heavily by his side. Time stood still.

Finally, Combs grinned. "I always knew you was cold-footed, Coulter. Now, I'm givin' ya one more chance — go on and do what you're told!"

Matt swallowed, and pretended not to hear the muffled chuckles of some of the others behind him as he reined his horse toward the store.

McKee didn't say anything as they walked their mounts up the rise. The silence was heavy.

Matt told himself that, all things concerned, he had done right. He had *tried* to talk Combs out of it. But since he couldn't, it was best to go through with it. He'd be especially careful and make sure they didn't hurt the old man in the store.

Moments later, Matt, followed by McKee, stepped inside the small building. Matt drew his Colt.

"Mister Walters, we gotta take your money." Matt made himself say it.

Walters looked up and saw them. His hands shook. Matt thought of Combs, waiting down by the creek, and considered the choice before him. It was either take the old man's money — at the worst, clubbing him lightly with his pistol — or face Combs.

The decision should be easy. A deadly showdown with Combs didn't make sense. Besides, now wasn't the right time to change his ways. Maybe after they got to Oklahoma Territory. Maybe . . . .

But somehow he was seeing Zeke Walters for the first time. He no longer was just a bony and stooped old man; the face had something about it — a gentleness, a look of kindness; the look of a man who would do something nice for someone else. Especially, most likely, for a boy.

Matt suddenly hated what he was doing. And the hate was far keener than any pain he had ever known; it was a bitterness in his mouth, a sickness in his stomach.

"What ya waitin' on, Matt?" McKee nudged him from behind.

It was then Matt knew this was one robbery he wouldn't go through with — didn't *have* to go through with.

He holstered his gun. "I was just funnin', Mister Walters. Guess it wasn't much of a joke. We just stopped by and ... Well, we wondered if maybe we could have a cup of coffee."

Relief filled Walters' watery eyes. "Why ... Why, you sure can, young fella!" He looked for a moment at the pistol, now at Matt's side, then at Matt's hand, now extended toward him. "And I'm ... I'm much obliged. The wife's been sick, and . . . ."

It was a look Matt knew he wouldn't forget. "No, sir," he said, "You got it wrong. It's *me* that's obliged to *you.*"

Later, outside, McKee shook his head as they mounted their horses. "I can't figure you, Coulter. Are you forgettin' how Del came near killin' you back there? When he sees ya didn't get the money, what ya gonna tell 'im?"

"I guess I'll just tell 'im *adios.*" Matt felt lifted by his own words. "I've made up my mind. I've pulled my last holdup."

"You crazy? You won't go nowhere when Del sees you went against 'im. He'll kill you sure as the devil!"

"He might," Matt said. "But then, maybe not. Maybe I'm as handy with a gun as he is. Besides, life ends soon for everybody — especially outlaws. And maybe dyin' ain't so bad, if a man dies for a reason."

"What? If ya ask me, you're talkin' loco. And tell me somethin' — why didn't ya take that old man's money, instead of drinkin' coffee and visitin' with 'im the way you did? You acted like he was a friend of yours or somethin'. Was he?"

Matt loosened his Colt in its holster and reined his horse toward the creek. "That's right, he was. A good friend I had once. A long time ago."

This is another reference to crime in Indian Territory, which also symbolizes Oklahoma's interesting mixture of cultures, as well as both good and evil. It is based specifically on a famous death sentence in Old West history. The story first appeared in 2003 in the book "Black Hats," edited by Robert J. Randisi and published by Berkley Books.

A Stay for a Badman

Young Crawford Goldsby felt the noose being slipped over his head, and for an instant recalled something his mother once told him: "Boy, I pray and pray that someday you'll change. You got nothin' but hate all bunched up inside you."

He stood on the gallows, handcuffed and shackled, his arms and legs bound with ropes, his face covered, before one of the largest crowds at a Fort Smith execution. They were here to see the hanging of Indian Territory's most notorious outlaw, "Cherokee Bill."

Well, she was right. And he would keep on hating right up to the end – if they expected him to cower and act remorseful, they could all go to hell. Following the reading of the death warrant and before the black hood was placed over his head, he had shunned the marshal's offer to say some last words. "I came here to die, not to make a speech!" he snapped.

Then he refused to listen to further words of the priest, Father Pius. He jerked his head away. "Let's get on with it."

Moments earlier, as he was accompanied to the scaffold by the party including his mother, Ellen Beck Lynch, and his colored "aunty," Amanda Foster, who helped raise him, he knew for certain his death sentence was final.

An execution ordered by Isaac Charles Parker, U.S. judge for the Western District of Arkansas – the "Hanging Judge" – was rarely deferred in the final hour. But he, like all the condemned men in the crowded, stinking prison underneath the courthouse, had held onto faint hopes for a stay. While Cherokee Bill was known to be tough as iron, he was also human and would welcome a chance to keep living, even if only until a later execution date.

And now, despite his bluster, his hands, cuffed behind him, trembled as if by their own will. Sweat stung his eyes inside the hood, even in the sunny but mild March afternoon – to everyone else, a beautiful, tranquil day. Warm wetness trickled down one of his legs. Any second, the trap would spring.

"But Mama, don't you remember something else you told me one time? You said for me never to let nobody run over me," Crawford had responded to his mother that time. It was during one of his rare visits to her, more than five years after he left home. It was early morning before daylight, and they sat at the kitchen table of the small house in Fort Gibson, talking as they sipped coffee.

"And that's just what I done, Mama – I didn't let that man run over me. Leastwise, I didn't let 'im get away with it. And ain't nobody gonna run over me again. Not ever!" He tilted back his chair and reached the Winchester he had leaned against the wall a good yard behind him. He gave the rifle a loving pat, and grinned and winked.

At eighteen years, Crawford Goldsby had a smooth olive complexion and keen, handsome features, and the generally dark countenance and curly black hair that bespoke his mixed racial background. His build was solid and his movements agile, which gave him the character of full maturity and self-assurance.

But the incident he spoke of was his most bitter memory. It had been several weeks since the night of the dance, when he had taken the beating of his life, but he could still taste blood and feel the pain of a smashed nose – and deep humiliation.

It was the happiest moment ever as he and pretty little Maggie Glass sat talking and sipping punch at the Fort Gibson social affair. But then he was forced to protect her from the drunken advances of Jake Lewis, an older man who was a known troublemaker and good with his fists, and they wound up outside. Crawford had been beaten, kicked, and left lying senseless in the mud.

A few days later he got hold of a six-shooter and went to where Lewis worked outside a livery barn and shot the man twice, and jumped on his horse and galloped off.

Lewis lived, though badly wounded, but from that moment on, Crawford had dodged the law and taken up with other wanted men who lived on the scout here and there within the Indian Nations.

"But, Crawford," his mother said, leaning toward him in her pleading way, "I didn't mean for you to go out and shoot somebody, and then start runnin' with bad people, and stealin' and mistreatin' decent folks – folks that never done you no harm. You was a good little boy at one time. And, Lord knows, I thought goin' to Indian school all that time would do you a world of good. But it seemed like overnight you just growed up and turned plumb mean."

"Them Indian schools wasn't that nice, Mama – leastwise, not for me. I got pushed around some there, because I wasn't very big then. And some of 'em called me names. They said I wasn't Indian – they called me bad names like 'nigger.'"

"I know, son, but what I mean is, you shouldn't have all that hate bunched up inside you. You don't have to hate every livin' soul around you. If you could only have a tender *feelin'* for somebody – repent, ask forgiveness of somebody you've done wrong. It's like the Good Book says, havin' the right feelin' will bring you salvation."

"I'll get my salvation with this, Mama," he said, slapping his Winchester again. With that he got up to leave. "I gotta be goin' – it's comin' daylight and there'll be folks in the streets. Besides that, it's about time for that man to finish up milkin' and sloppin' the hogs. Me and him don't have nothin' to talk about."

Crawford and his stepfather, William Lynch, had never gotten along. That was one reason Crawford had left home about a year after he got home from school, and gone up to near Nowata to live with his sister, Georgia, and her husband, Mose Brown.

Ellen Beck begged her son to stay for breakfast. But he didn't answer as he opened the door and cautiously looked out. The town was scattered around a stockade that until a few years before had been a busy Army post. Save for a few rooster crows, the community still lay quiet in the first rays of the sun. He quickly stepped to his

Crawford "Cherokee Bill" Goldsby.
Western History Collections,
University of Oklahoma Libraries.

horse, jammed the rifle into the saddle boot, mounted, and rode off, keeping the animal at a brisk but quiet walk.

It was a few days later when Crawford and his two partners, brothers Bill and Jim Cook, who were also part Cherokee, decided to collect their "Cherokee Strip" money. There would be payments issued to legitimate tribal members from the government's purchase from the tribe of the Cherokee Outlet. More than $6 million was to be paid to the Cherokees, with every tribal member listed as having sufficient Cherokee blood to receive slightly more than $265.

But to get theirs, Crawford and the Cooks would have to send someone for it, as they knew they would be arrested when seen in public by officers. So, along with two others, Jess Cochran and Jim French, they holed up for a few days at the Halfway House, a stage stop and road ranch of sorts between Tahlequah and Wagoner, two important locations in the Cherokee Nation.

The establishment, at the top of a slope a short piece up from the small stream of Fourteen Mile Creek, was also known as a den for whiskey smugglers and other wrongdoers. Effie Crittenden, the proprietor, a fiery little woman with somewhat of a tough reputation of her own, agreed to go to Tahlequah and get their money on the designated day.

Effie got back with the money, but a posse of lawmen would soon be on her trail.

Leaders of the Cherokee Lighthorse and other officers had gotten wind of the outlaws' whereabouts, and saw it as the opportunity to nab the two fugitives – Crawford Goldsby, wanted for shooting Lewis, and Jim Cook, charged with stealing a horse.

Shortly after noon on Sunday, June 17, 1894 – the day after Effie Crittenden collected the money for Crawford and the Cook brothers – the posse, led by Ellis Rattling Gourd, chief of the Cherokee Lighthorse, rode out from the Cherokee National Capitol in Tahlequah. Riding with Rattling Gourd were Sequoyah Houston, a tribal deputy sheriff and a member of the Lighthorse; and brothers Dick and E.C.

"Zeke" Crittenden, both known as gunfighters. Others in the party were Bill Bracket, Bill McKee, Isaac Grease, George Parris, Bob Woodall and Nelson Hicks.

A few hours later at the Halfway House, Crawford and his partners had finished eating a leisurely meal and were sitting around smoking and discussing plans. They were getting too well-known in the Nations, they said, so might head down to Texas, or maybe west, all the way through Oklahoma Territory and into New Mexico.

But a shout from outside threw the room into a hush. "You in the house, we got you covered. Throw down your guns and come out, and with your hands up!" It sounded like Rattling Gourd. They all knew him.

In seconds, they were in defensive positions, both inside and outside the frame structure, all armed. Even Effie, though planning to stay out of the fight, had her pistol handy in case she needed it. Crawford, who by now was a crack shot with both six-shooter and his Winchester, stood outside and peered around the corner, the rifle cocked.

Nearly twenty minutes crept by in deafening silence. The men in and around the building couldn't see anyone, but reasoned the posse had to be across the clearing and in the blackjack timber where the rocky hill began sloping down toward the creek, the easiest and most logical approach to their location. It was a good distance, but within firing range. Sweating in the afternoon heat, and hearing only the occasional twitter of a mockingbird or the buzzing of a horsefly, the men waited, their Winchesters and pistols ready.

In a sudden surprise, one of the lawmen stood up from his brushy cover and called out, "Come on out, boys. Let's keep this peaceful" – and nearly in the same instant, Crawford caught the man in his rifle sights and fired. The lawman vanished as if by magic as the shot seemed to echo through the surrounding blackjacks and even the tall cottonwoods and sycamores down by the creek.

The fight was on. Guns popped and cracked both in the woods and in and around the frame building, the smoke at times so thick the woods were barely visible, and the air sharp with burning gunpowder. Lead slugs whined off rocks

The late Mack Houston of Tahlequah, during 1971 visit to the grave of his father, Sequoyah Houston, who was killed by Cherokee Bill.

and whacked into the old wood of the Halfway House.

Crawford barely caught the words of one of the posse above the clatter of gunfire, "Sequoyah's been hit!"

A pang of regret seized him, and a sickness welled from deep in his stomach. The man he shot was Sequoyah Houston! He remembered him from when he was small. The man was one of the few grown-ups to treat him well, sometimes playing his fiddle and telling funny stories for him and a few other youngsters. He also taught Crawford many things about the woods, like how to hunt and shoot, and how to make whistles out of hickory branches.

And Crawford had shot the man square in the chest. He knew he had most likely killed one of the few friends he ever had.

The fight raged. A few yards from Crawford, one of his partners screamed and dropped his rifle. It was Jim Cook. He stood bleeding, his face twisted in pain.

After a time, fewer shots were coming from the posse, which was a relief to Crawford and the others as the sun had lowered and was now blinding them with its glare. It looked like several of the posse had left. The best Crawford could tell, there were only two shooters remaining in the woods – he guessed the Crittenden brothers, who, eager gunfighters that they were, likely would be the last to quit fighting.

He also reasoned that most of the posse had left to take the injured Houston for help – most likely to the small store operated by Xerxes "Zack" Taylor, and wife, Jennie, not far from the creek.

Crawford hated what he had done but now could do nothing but fight back, along with the rest of his bunch, until they could manage to get to their horses in the barn behind them and scatter. The timber in that direction was thick and the hill steep and rocky, but it was their only chance. And now was their best time to go, before the other lawmen could return.

"If only I had known it was Sequoyah shooting at that

house, I wouldn't have fired!" Bill said to himself and would later say over and over to his partners. But a bullet couldn't be taken back, and it did no good at all to keep thinking about it.

Before they could withdraw from the battle, Jim Cook yelled. He was hit again, this time, it seemed, in the shoulder, on the same side where he was shot the first time. He had been firing his pistol with his good hand as his other arm, soaked with blood, dangled, when he was hit again. But this time it apparently was with buckshot – which, at the distance, wouldn't do near as much damage as rifle or even pistol – so Crawford was hopeful he wouldn't slow them down in their retreat. He didn't aim to get caught.

One or two at a time, and with Jim Cook being helped along, all five finally got to their horses and rode down the rough hillside, the tangles of thick growth clawing at their faces, and their mounts stumbling over rocks.

They soon scattered and all got clean away, except for the injured Jim Cook, who would be captured two days later where he lay wounded in a pasture near Fort Gibson.

And Crawford would soon learn that the gun battle had given him a nickname –one by which he would become famous. When officers questioned Effie Crittenden immediately after the shoot-out, she was asked if one of the men was Crawford Goldsby. And, while her answer was never explained, to Goldsby or anyone else, she answered, "No, it was 'Cherokee Bill.'"

Residents throughout both Indian and Oklahoma territories, as well as some elsewhere, would learn, from newspapers and other reports, much about the outlaw known as Cherokee Bill – who had a background not altogether typical of a desperado.

It was said he was born in Fort Concho, Texas, and was the son of George Goldsby, a "buffalo soldier," who gained the rank of sergeant major before his military career was ruined by trouble involving a dispute between soldiers and civilians. His mother, as Ellen Beck, was born in Indian Territory and was the descendant of slaves.

Crawford Goldsby was believed to be part Sioux Indian and Cherokee Indian, with a background of Mexican as well as Negro. It was said he had a confused life as a boy, being sent to the two Indian schools, first at Cherokee, Kansas, for three years, then at the Carlisle Indian Industrial School in Pennsylvania for two years, followed by heated arguments with his stepfather.

Until he met Maggie Glass, his mother was the only person he loved, despite some bitterness he felt toward her for sending him away to school – although he had come to realize she had only done her best, as it was hard for her to care for him and his sister, Georgia, and two brothers, Clarence and Luther.

Cherokee Bill gained notoriety both on his won and as a member of the "Cook Gang" of outlaws, which soon after the Halfway House shoot-out went on a spree of robbing trains, stagecoaches, banks and post offices throughout parts of both Indian and Oklahoma territories, and even getting chased out of Texas and New Mexico by lawmen.

Along with Bill Cook, Cherokee Bill, and Jim French, the gang was believed to have grown to include Sam McWilliams, also known as "the Verdigris Kid"; and at least three others: Lon Gordon, Henry Munson and Curtis Dayson.

The gang threw such panic across much of Indian Territory that, in addition to the posting of rewards for the capture of any or all the members, authorities wired the Office of Indian Affairs in Washington for help; and federal lawmen at Fort Smith acknowledged they didn't have enough funds or field deputies to corral the outlaws. Washington officials even threatened to abrogate the Indian treaties and establish a territorial government.

By his own deeds, Cherokee Bill was dubbed by writers as "the fiercest of the Cook Gang" and "the quickest man in the Territory with a gun."

Thunder in the Heartland

He would eventually be blamed for killing three men, his brother-in-law Mose Brown, reportedly during a dispute over hogs; Ernest Melton, an innocent bystander during a store robbery by Bill and another gang member in Lenapah; and Lawrence Keating, a guard in the federal jail in Fort Smith. Bill shot the guard after managing to have a smuggled revolver in his cell.

Unofficially, Cherokee Bill was credited with a number of murders that occurred during the Cook Gang's hold-ups and various scrapes. Some observers said he killed as many as fourteen men.

It was Cherokee Bill's love for Maggie Glass – along with the trickery of an acquaintance, Ike Rogers, who also held a deputy marshal's commission – that brought about Bill's capture. With Bill, along with the unsuspecting Maggie, as a guest in Rogers' cabin near Nowata, Rogers and another man, after a hard struggle, managed to get Cherokee Bill into handcuffs.

Judge Parker would set the execution date for Crawford Goldsby as Tuesday, March 17, 1896. And that's when, after nearly a year behind bars during which Goldsby attempted a jailbreak and killed the guard, the outlaw known as Cherokee Bill would die on the gallows, at age twenty.

The hanging ceremony was taking longer than Crawford expected. Since he'd had almost a year to think, he realized there were only two men in the world he hated – Jake Lewis, whom he considered the cause of all his trouble, and Ike Rogers, who had betrayed him.

Which meant he had killed some that he didn't hate – didn't even dislike. Among them was the first man he killed, Sequoyah Houston, a kind man who had befriended him. He hadn't known he was shooting at Sequoyah that time at the Halfway House, but that didn't make him feel better.

There were others, too, like his sister's husband, Mose. He hadn't liked the man, but he wished he hadn't shot him down over a small disagreement. And Ernest Melton, who happened to be standing in the wrong place during the robbery in Lenapah. He had nothing against the prison guard, either, other than his being a lawman.

Why he had all those feelings now, he didn't know – it was like his many regrets, long kept hidden from even himself, now gushed out into the open.

His mother was wrong in thinking he had no sorrowful feelings about anything. Probably the worst of his regrets, in fact, was that it was too late to tell her how he really felt – to give her that one little bit of comfort before he died – especially since she was the only person still alive to whom all that would matter.

And now the only way he could do that — the only way he could *possibly* do that – was to say he was sorry. And to say it to his mother, if there was a way in Heaven's name he could!

He *was* truly sorry for the many wrong things he had done, and would give anything if he could let her know that. He didn't mind dying at all – if only he could die knowing that at least his mother knew how he felt.

Crawford knew then that he *had* to tell her! He would die happily if he could only, somehow, send his last thought to her first.

Maybe if he wished strongly enough, he might communicate – maybe he could make his thoughts fly to where she stood in the crowded courthouse yard, weeping and telling him her silent good-bye. Maybe he could, if his last thoughts were strong enough. Maybe . . .

"Mama, I'm sorry!" he actually heard himself call out, between sobs. "Please hear me. I love you, Mama!"

It was then that strange things began to happen.

The noose and hood were being removed, and Bill was jerked from his feverish thoughts by the brightness, and he was instantly back into what was going on at the moment.

He blinked against the sunlight, and the marshal, who was still holding the hood, smiled at him. He blinked again.

Somehow, there had been a stay. He was free! His

mother was right! He had expressed his feelings, and it had brought his salvation.

Within minutes, he was riding away. He had never felt so uplifted. The day was bright and sunny, but there was no glare to hurt his eyes, and no sweaty heat. His horse went at a fast, easy gait, which raised no dust.

Strange as it seemed, he realized he was riding toward his boyhood home, where both Maggie and his mother were waiting for him. He would greet his mother first, and tell her what he wanted to say. He could hardly wait to see her, and to feel her hug him the way she did when he was small.

The executioner, the physician and two deputy marshals were astonished as the body was removed from underneath the gallows.

"He sure don't look like the mean one that he was, does he?" one of the deputies said.

"No, I never seen one of 'em look so peaceful," the other said. "Except for his broke neck, he looks like a sleepin' child."

This portrayal of fictitious cowboys shortly before 1900 is a tribute to the Great Western Trail, as well as to Oklahoma's two traditionally major agricultural products: beef cattle and wheat. It was first in print in 1994 in the book, New Trails — 23 Original Stories of the West, *edited by John Jakes and Martin H. Greenberg, and published by Doubleday.*

Yearlings

It was the most important cattle drive of J.T. McCoy's life. Partly because he felt sure it would be his last, but mainly because his son, Jed, had come with him, and this was his last chance to make the boy into what he ought to be.

McCoy, a weathered, stout man in his late fifties, rode apart from the others, aware of the smell of the sagebrush and the long shadows of the yucca shoots in the freshness of early morning, a hawk floating against the blue sky, the squeak of saddle leather, and the soft clop of his horse. The scuffle of the cattle ahead raised just shy of enough dust to spoil the whole pretty picture.

Funny, he thought with a pang, how a man starts noticing life all around him when he's near the end of it. And that made him start worrying again about Jed.

Another horse galloped up and slowed beside his, and he glanced over to see his son, a skinny but friendly, handsome youth of twenty-one who was holding awkwardly onto the saddle horn until his pony came down out of its rough trot.

He flashed a boyish grin. "Pretty morning, isn't it? I'm sure glad I came with you, Papa."

J.T. felt a surge of warmth, but showed it with only a thin smile. "I am too, Son. You gotta remember, though, it'll be hot before the day's over, and you can't let that keep you from stayin' close behind these calves. We can't let any get scattered and lost before we get 'em loaded."

"Don't worry, Papa, we'll get all of them there. And I'm glad to be here helping you," the young man said.

He pointed to one of several bare, red hills up ahead. "See that big mound over there? When we're in camp to-night I'm gonna draw a picture of it and put you and your horse right on top of it. And have a few clouds overhead and . . . ."

J.T. breathed out in a tired gesture. "Son, we just don't have time for thinkin' about pretty pictures. What me and you both gotta keep our minds on in the next few days is these eighty-five head of cattle."

"I've been wanting to ask you about that," Jed said. "I don't know as much as you do, but wouldn't it be better to keep more of your younger animals, especially the females?"

J.T. was surprised by the boy's interest. So he'd explain, even if he weren't happy about it. "That's right, Son, it would be better – if things was the way I'd like 'em to be. Most of these are yearlin' steers and heifers that I'd like to keep and graze out this summer, and use some of the females for breedin' stock. But the way times are now, as dry as it's been and with some extra expenses I've had lately, we need every pound we can take to market."

"That's something else," Jed said. "Have you ever thought about giving the cattle something else to eat? What I mean is, I've studied a little about alfalfa and wheat and . . . And this girl from Kansas I know – I've been wanting to tell you about her anyway, Papa – her folks farm and raise cattle, too. And they . . . ."

"I don't care what farmers do, Jed! You should know that. I'm a rancher, just like my father was, and I hope that's what you'll be. By Heavens, hard luck or not, I'm gonna do whatever I have to do to keep ranchin'. Our land's always goin' to raise cattle, not crops — as long as I'm alive."

Jed didn't say anything, and J.T. brooded. Not only did the boy have a lot to learn — he had to start thinking like a cattleman. Maybe this little drive would help.

After a few minutes he said, "Here's another thing. The sooner we get there, the better chance we have of gettin' a decent price. I aim to cross the Canadian with 'em today and have 'em at the railroad by day after tomorrow."

"Besides," he added, and grinned, "if we get as far as we oughta get today, you'll be too tired tonight to do any drawin', I'll guarantee ya that."

"You've been on lots of drives, haven't you, Papa?"

"Sure have, Son. And takin' cattle to market sure has changed. This little trip don't amount to nothin', compared to the way it used to be."

Jed wouldn't understand, of course, how western Oklahoma Territory had changed, since all he knew was the present, and the coming start of the twentieth century.

Now, he and Jed and their neighbors, Woodrow Cline and his sons, only had to drive their combined herd of about two-hundred mixed cattle for only three or four days to the railroad at Woodward. It was nothing like the big drives from Texas to Kansas that as recent as five years or so ago were still coming right through this part of the country.

It was one of those drives, J.T. recalled in an instant, which took his father's life less than thirty years ago. He wished again he could blot out the nightmarish picture he saw over and over of his father's drowning.

J.T. was one of the hands on the drive that was crossing the rain-swollen Red River — and watched in horror from a few yards away as his father, who was trail boss, was swept from his saddle by the currents and swallowed by the nasty-red swirls. J.T. jumped from his horse to grab him, but failed — then got his own lungs full of water and had to be dragged out by the others.

J.T.'s father had ranched in South Texas long before he began taking his herds north over the Great Western Trail, and had fought everything from renegade Indians and gun-toting cattle and horse thieves to spells so dry the cows choked on dust and lived on mesquite beans and prickly pear cactus.

Following his father's death, J.T. had begun making arrangements to graze cattle up in the usually lush grasslands of the Indian country.

And finally, eight years ago, he and his small family had made the run and homesteaded in the Cheyenne and Arapaho lands — but to raise cattle, not farm like many settlers did. It was fine country, overall, and after living in a dugout for a while he had built a decent house.

But during a hard winter a few years later, his wife, Priscilla, died of pneumonia. Life for him and Jed became not only difficult, as neither was any count at housekeeping or cooking, but painfully lonely.

A few years later came the dry spell, over much of Texas and the Territory too, and many cattlemen started reducing their herds, bringing down the price of beef.

Then about six months ago, J.T. became aware of a change taking place in his body. Pains came and went, and sometimes were too severe to ignore. He had gone to a doctor in Cheyenne — the first physician he had ever consulted — then to another doctor over in Canadian in the Texas Panhandle. Then still another out in Amarillo. All three said it was something they called "terminal." There was medicine he could take for the pain, but it would continue to worsen until the end — which could come within a year, maybe a little later.

J.T., who considered himself tough enough to handle about any kind of trouble, accepted the idea, but hadn't seen any reason to tell Jed until he had to.

And now, since ranching had always been his life, as his father's before him, his biggest aim was to do a good job of passing his land, cattle, and all his knowledge to his son.

Thunder in the Heartland

But Jed, while a decent, well-mannered lad who was eager to please, couldn't seem to do anything right. Making him into a rancher wouldn't be easy. The boy couldn't handle a lariat rope without it twisting — and even if he could, he had a hard time staying on a horse that was fast enough to catch a calf. And when he put the branding iron to a calf, he'd turn his head and flinch.

When he was little, he was always running off to go swimming in the Washita River or in the first stock tank he came to.

And worse, when he was older, he usually wasn't around for ranch work because he was off reading books, or just wandering, drawing pictures.

Also, the boy had talked him into letting him go away to a school in Missouri. Even though Jed worked at some odd jobs to help out, the expense on J.T. was an extra burden.

And a few weeks ago, Jed came home – to stay and help run the ranch, J.T. hoped. But the boy said he also was going to be a professional artist — and J.T. hadn't been able to convince him that didn't make sense.

Woodrow Cline trotted up on his horse, grinning in his big bucktoothed way.

J.T. and Jed had known Cline and his two fun-loving boys, Melvin and Andrew, who were both a little younger than Jed, ever since they had come to the Territory. They often partnered with them when working and moving their cattle. They were fine neighbors.

At that moment, one of the larger animals in the herd, a part-longhorn, cantankerous steer owned by the Clines, stopped and slung his head, then bolted, heading off to the right toward some shinnery bushes.

"That ol' steer's the orneriest thing you ever saw when you try to drive 'im out of brush," Cline said. "One of these boys might oughta go rope 'im."

Melvin and Andrew were bringing back a few strays to

the left of the herd and were out of earshot — and the two men glanced toward Jed.

J.T. watched his son hesitate, then shake out his coiled rope and spur his pony into a lope. In minutes, he was closing in on the steer with his loop swinging.

"Git 'im, Jed!" Cline hollered.

J.T. stood up in his stirrups and watched.

The steer wheeled just before reaching the shinnery, and Jed threw the lasso. His loop dropped neatly over an idle tumbleweed about the time the long-legged critter was several jumps away and heading straight for a brushy canyon.

Jed's horse, meanwhile, had slid to a stop the moment Jed swung the rope. Jed flew over the saddle's tall pommel and hung by one arm around the pony's neck.

A chorus of laughter and good-natured shouts of derision arose from the Cline boys — who now were galloping over to get into the action. Jed, red-faced, eased himself to the ground and joined in with a joking excuse about how the steer was too dumb to know he was supposed to stick his head in the loop.

But J.T. wasn't having fun. He fixed Jed with the cold stare he had often given him over the years. Then he reined his horse off in the other direction.

"Sorry, Papa," Jed called after him. "I'll get back on and go drive him back."

"Let 'im go," J.T. said tiredly, rolling his eyes toward the sky. Then he called out to the Cline brothers. "Mel! Andrew! You boys better go bring that wild hombre in. This ol' pony Jed's ridin' has a bad leg."

"Sorry, Papa," Jed said again.

The Cline brothers took off together, their ropes whirring and their horses, with ears back, in a dead run. The riders went out of sight over a rise and in moments returned, their ponies thundering only a few yards behind the steer.

"Yah-hooooo!" yelled Woodrow. "They're puttin' on a regular ropin' show, ain't they?"

Andrew threw his loop, which grazed but failed to catch one of the horns as the steer slung its head.

Mel's loop shot out and tightened around the base of the steer's horns, and in nearly the same instant his stocky dun jerked the animal around and to a snorting, angry standstill.

"Ya see, Andrew, that's how ya do it. Want me to do it again so you can watch real close this time?" the youth hollered.

"Lucky, ain't ya? Too bad you're so bashful when it comes to talkin' about yourself, too," Andrew said. He gathered his rope.

"Don't get ya bristles up, Andrew," the senior Cline said. "Remember, like they say over in Texas, 'If you can do it, it ain't braggin'.'"

"Let's turn 'im loose and try again," Andrew yelled to his brother. "I'll bet ya two bits I'll beat ya this time!"

But Cline, though still grinning, called an end to it. "That's enough, boys. No use runnin' any more fat off these hides than we have to."

"They're right smart hands, Woodrow," J.T. said with a smile, trying to keep the disappointment in his own son out of his voice for Cline's benefit — and not caring much whether he failed to for Jed's.

"Yeah, but I gotta keep a tight rein on 'em," Cline said. "Them boys of mine are just yearlin's. They don't know much, but maybe they'll grow up one of these days."

The drive during most of the afternoon was slow, hot, and dry. The drought, which was like some he had seen in South Texas, was more and more on J.T.'s mind, and in what little conversation went on between him and Woodrow.

Big, fluffy clouds with dark undersides built to their west over the Texas Panhandle and gave the herders some refreshing diversion — but little hope for rain. Cloud banks this time of year didn't always mean moisture.

Jed was looking in his dreamy way at the heavenly display, which J.T. had to admit was pretty — starkly white, billowy masses suspended against the blue sky. He knew his son was studying every detail, thinking of a painting.

But to J.T. and the others, the clouds only meant what likely were false promises. Like when one of the clouds moved past the sun, its broad, welcome shadow spread over them — then all too soon flowed across the prairie and was gone.

The hot afternoon dragged on, the time passing as slowly as the plodding of the herd – until, at nearly sundown, the cattle and horses smelled the Canadian River.

The cattle began stepping. J.T., Jed and Woodrow Cline rode around the herd to get a look at the river and find a good crossing. Melvin and Andrew stayed back and on either side of the cattle.

"Ya know, I might even take me a bath," Woodrow said as the three, standing in the stirrups, went at a long trot. J.T. and Jed both laughed. All were excited about what was ahead.

That's when they heard the roar.

"Now don't tell me the river's rollin'!" said Woodrow, wearing one of his few serious looks. All three lifted their horses into a lope. "If it is, it musta rained a bunch out in the Panhandle in the last day or two."

Sure enough, the river was rising. And the roaring, now much louder, was coming from upstream.

"It's amazing, isn't it?" Jed said. "I've heard about people actually hearing a river flood coming, even before they could see it. But I never thought it possible."

J.T., though, saw it differently.

He had been thrown from a few horses, been in a bruising saloon fight or two, been bitten below the knee by a rattler, and even had a tooth pulled without benefit of liquor. He figured he was as brave as the next man. But he had forgotten his uncontrollable fear of flooding rivers — the rushing, nasty, stinking, muddy water with its whirlpools and scummy edges that turned up bodies of drowned varmints and sometimes even calves.

Maybe he had spouted off too soon when he said they'd cross the river this same day. He hadn't considered the possibility of high water, rare in this country, especially during dry periods. Too late now, he thought. The thirsty cattle were trotting around them on their way to the water. Some already crowded at the muddy edge.

"Think we can push 'em across before it gets too high?" asked Woodrow, looking to J.T. for the answer.

But for once, J.T. didn't have one. "Well, I don't know much about rivers. It looks mighty high to me already."

"I think we can do it, Papa," Jed put in — to J.T.'s surprise. "The cattle are still thirsty and maybe they won't stop to think about it. We'll have to hurry, though."

"I bet he's right, J.T.," Woodrow said. "That way, we can get 'em across before dark — and before the river's any higher." He gave a whoop and waved his coiled lariat. "Come on, fellers, let's put 'em in!"

One of J.T.'s pains hit him, and his heart skipped a beat or two. But he lifted his reins and gently spurred his horse, shutting his eyes as the cool water came above his boot tops.

Despite his will, his body revolted. He wheeled his horse around and plunged it through the water back toward dry land. "I can't do it!" he heard himself yell.

Back on the bank, he slid from his saddle, and didn't look up.

It was Jed who spoke. "Well, the river *is* rising fast, and it's nearly dark. We might have a better chance in the morning. And it might drop some by that time."

J.T. was grateful to his son. It made him feel odd.

They all ate their beef jerky, raisins and cold biscuits and drank coffee made from canteen water. Then they rolled out their bedding and went quickly to sleep on the ground.

Except for J.T.

He lay listening to the rushing water. While he hated the prospect of dying a lingering death in bed, he knew he wanted to go any other way but drowning. And now, he was in an even worse predicament. He had ridden herd on his son for years because of his weaknesses, and now he knew what he'd do tomorrow when he entered the river again. In his brief contact with it today, he had gone as crazy as a wild cow in a thunderstorm.

He didn't know which he feared more — drowning in the muddy water, or seeing his son humiliated by his father. Funny, for the first time since he learned of his illness, that wasn't his biggest worry.

It was even funnier, he thought — this time giving himself a twisted smile — this was one time he wasn't worried about how *Jed* was going to perform.

J.T. dozed off and on, but morning still came too quickly, and in moments all were up, drinking the coffee Woodrow Cline had boiled over a fire, eating jerky and preparing for a big day.

J.T. looked at the river, and turned sick. It was fuller than before, roaring something awful, rushing by in filthy, reddish foam that carried brush and logs.

"Well, ready to try it, fellers?" Woodrow said.

J.T. didn't answer him. How anyone so silly-looking could be so cussed brave, he'd never know.

It was clear no one felt real confident. But soon J.T. and Jed — since they had taken the lead yesterday, they were expected to today — went first, wading their horses slowly out into the water. Once they crossed, the others would push the herd behind them.

J.T. wasn't going to turn back as he did the day before — even if it meant drowning. He clinched his teeth and shut his eyes as he again felt the cold water, more chilling this time, reach his knees — then in a breathtaking instant rush to his armpits as he sensed his horse's feet leave the bottom of the river.

The water rose to his chin and his body floated awkwardly up and out of the saddle. He could see only the animal's head above the water and a few inches in front of his own. He swallowed a mouthful of water and coughed.

"Jed! Where are you? Help me!" He could barely hear

his own words. The river was a deafening monster that swept him in a blur past the trees and everything else he could see on the far bank. He turned his face skyward to keep his nose out of the water, and prayed.

As the main current hit him, his horse went sideways. He heard Jed yell for him to hold on. But the horse's reins and mane slipped from his hand, and he lost sight of daylight and sank into the blurry, choking world of dirty water. In a spasm of gagging and coughing, he clawed at the water, feeling his head bob above the surface for an instant at a time. He knew he was drowning — until his right hand caught a rope that jerked him half out of the water.

"Papa! Hang on! Keep your face out of the water when you can — and stay calm!" It was Jed. He was off his horse and in the water, too, swimming a few yards ahead. It all was confusing. "Keep your head up, and kick your feet! And when your face goes under, hold your breath." Jed kept yelling. And every time J.T. started sinking again, Jed would jerk the rope.

His voice was now easier to hear above the roar. They had reached a little bend where the current no longer hit them full blast.

J.T. blinked away some of the blur and saw the bank a short distance past Jed, and in a few seconds felt his feet touch the muddy bottom. It was a miracle, he told himself. An absolute miracle!

They waded toward the bank in calmer, shallower water. J.T. stopped coughing and found his voice. "I thought I was a goner — and I would've been if it wasn't for you, Son. You saved my life!"

"I didn't do it all, Papa. When I saw you come off your horse, I went off, too, and swam a little ahead of you and threw you my rope — if I'd let you grab my hand, you might have drowned us both. If you hadn't stayed calm and done exactly like I told you, I couldn't have pulled you out."

"Water's nothing to be afraid of, unless you fight it,"

---

he added. "That's probably what happened to my grandpa that time in the Red River."

"I won't be doin' this again, I'll guarantee ya that!" J.T. said. "In fact, Jed, I been plannin' on tellin' ya this. Maybe it'd been just as well if I had've stayed under water. You see, I'm dyin' — chances are, I don't have many months left."

"I figured that, Papa. I knew something was wrong when I heard you went to all those doctors. That's why I came home to help with the drive. But let's don't worry about that till we have to. In the meantime, I'm here with you."

J.T. slopped out of the water, still hanging onto the rope. They climbed up the grassy bank, where Woodrow Cline and his two sons were standing, and all three cheering.

"You made it back, fellers — and both of ya'll was way out in the middle!" Woodrow's bucktoothed grin was a welcome sight.

"Wait a minute!" J.T. said, still spitting out river water and looking around, disoriented. "You mean we didn't make it across?"

"No, it was too swift," Jed said. "I thought it was to begin with, but thought maybe we could make it; I should have known better. Then when we hit the main current, I knew all we could do was turn back."

"Besides," he said, "I figure this side of the river's the best place for us now anyway."

J.T. wasn't sure what his son meant, but still had some things he wanted to say. "Jed, no matter how you explained it, I wasn't worth two cents in that water — I'd be a drowned rat if it wasn't for you. It's funny how I used to get on ya for runnin' off and playin' in the water."

He looked down as he walked, his boots squishing, toward his grazing horse. "In fact, Jed, I guess you're man enough to be an artist or anything you wanna be. Looks like you're more grown up than I've been. I just couldn't seem to understand some things. As Woodrow would say, guess I've been actin' like a yearlin'."

He turned away from Jed like he had done many times

before, but this time it was because he didn't want his son to see his face. And he wanted to say more, but couldn't.

"Ah, Papa, you're way ahead of yourself," Jed said. "I'm going to be an artist, all right, because that's what I'm good at. I didn't tell you, but I've sold some of my paintings already — that's been my part-time job I told you about. But I never said that's all I'm going to do. I'll be painting pictures every now and then. After all, ranching isn't going to take *all* my time."

"You mean you're . . . ."

"That's right. In fact, I've got some ideas, like planting some alfalfa, and wheat, too — that's something cows can eat like grass right in the middle of wintertime. You see, you can still be a rancher, but it doesn't hurt to take a few ideas from the farmers."

"And as for now," he added, turning and looking at the grazing cattle, "that river's not going to go down as soon as we thought, and maybe that's just as well. We haven't come but about a third of the way to the railroad anyway, so — providing Mister Cline agrees with this — why don't we drive the herd back? Then maybe we can figure out a way to keep from selling right now — and maybe our yearling steers can get some more weight on them, and we can keep some of the females as replacement heifers."

J.T. wiped his face with his wet sleeve. "How in Heaven's name do you know about things like that?"

"I studied a few things besides art in school, Papa." Jed smiled, and went on. "Now, I know times are hard, but I believe if we don't get in a hurry to sell, and all get our heads together as one bigger outfit, we can survive. With what I've learned in school — and with your experience, and with expert cowmen like Mister Cline and Mel and Andrew, I'll bet we can make it."

"Ya know, I got a feelin' Jed's right, J.T.," Woodrow said, grinning bigger than normal. "Me and these boys of mine will sure enough do our part."

"And look," Jed added, nodding toward the river. "It's

been raining in the Panhandle, and that should mean the drought's over for us, too — so the buffalo grass should be greening up good even before we plant the alfalfa and wheat."

"Could be, Son," J.T. said thoughtfully. "Maybe you can make the ranch last longer than I will, anyway."

"That's another thing, Papa. None of us knows for sure what will happen tomorrow. And as strong as you look, I'll bet you live longer than you think – at least, long enough to see the first of your grandkids."

"Grandkids?"

"It's probably a good thing the river was too high to cross," Jed said. "That'll make us all go back and do something better than sell all our cattle when the price is down. Like Amy Lee always tells me, things sometime work out for the best."

"I don't know about all this, Jed. Besides, I ... 'Amy Lee'? Who in Heaven's name are you talking about?"

"I met Amy Lee at school. I tried to tell you about her before, but decided it wasn't a good time. Amy and I were married two weeks ago. I was going to send for her after this drive, but now that we're postponing that, I'll send for her right away. She's up in Kansas with her folks."

"She grew up there, by the way," he added, "and she knows probably more about cattle, and alfalfa and wheat — especially wheat — than I do. She'll be living on the ranch with us. She can sure cook, too."

This was the craziest cattle drive J.T. had ever been on. But maybe it was the best, come to think of it, even if the cattle weren't going anywhere this time except back home.

He looked again at the river, which was still roaring — but somehow it didn't seem as fearsome as it did. In a way, it was more like a friend. And he felt better than he had in years. But even if he died tomorrow, he thought, he couldn't complain too much.

Not that he planned on it. This drive had given him a whole new aim. J.T. knew now he had never really gotten to know his son — but that, by Heavens, it wasn't too late.

In the vicinity of the western tip of the Panhandle, shortly after the region became Oklahoma Territory, saloon proprietor Dan Brogan was fatally shot by one of two drunken cowboys. He is buried in the small Kenton cemetery – and is the inspiration for the following tale.

A Peaceful Life for Nat Lorraine

Now that he owned the small saloon, Nathan Lorraine felt as cozy as a rattlesnake in a prairie dog hole. It was only two rooms with a porch out at the lonely tip of the Panhandle, and didn't even have a name, but it drew thirsty ranch hands from miles around and meant a decent monthly income — even if roughly all of it came on a Saturday night. Lorraine figured that was enough to provide for his old age, and was mighty proud that he got lucky one day and bought the place for a little of nothing.

It was funny, too, how things turned out. Here he was, behind the bar at the same old watering hole where he used to blow his money when he was young and fool-headed.

Ever since Nat Lorraine realized he had too many years on him to keep hiring out as a cowboy, especially after a green colt got buggery when he was chasing a steer down the Mesa and gave him a bad fall, leaving him somewhat crippled, he had been troubled that the day was coming when he couldn't get by.

He even feared he might have to look up his long-lost daughter, and knew just how well that would set with her, and her husband — especially since Nat hadn't seen her since she was a little thing when he left her mama.

Until one hot afternoon when he had ridden by the saloon on his way to check a windmill and stopped to cool off on the shady porch and chew the fat with old Gabriel McFall. Old Gabe, who had run the place since way back when this part of Oklahoma Territory was No Man's Land, mentioned he was thinking of selling out — and Nat, joshing at first, offered a fourth of what McFall said it was worth, which wasn't a heck of a lot anyway. They bickered over the two figures until Nat said, "Well, Gabe, whatcha say let's cut the cards for it?" — and won. He bought the ramshackle old whiskey mill by barely scraping up the lower amount. If he

Early-day cattle roundup in the Black Mesa area. Photo courtesy, Bud Henry Davis.

had lost, all the old man could have done was cuss him out.

Now, Nat figured all he had to worry about was keeping the more rowdy galoots on Saturday nights from shooting the roof more full of holes than it was already. But most of the time, he could just sit back and enjoy the peace and quiet.

In fact, that was what he favored most about his new position. In wintertime he sipped coffee next to the little stove that hummed and popped while burning dead cottonwood and cedar, and during pretty weather he spent long hours in the rope-bottom chair out on the porch. That was where, of a morning, he watched the sunrise and looked for antelopes among the crooked fingers of walkingstick cactus and sharp-pointed bunches of soap weed; and late in the day looked for eagles that sometimes circled where summer's billowy clouds made shadows creep across Black Mesa. And he'd reminisce.

He had some good memories, too – along with others. Like any man in his sixties, he had done a few things he didn't enjoy recollecting.

When Nat had left his wife in Kansas to find work, neither of them was very content with their marriage, but he *did* aim to come back. But things happened — like his first trouble with the law — and time slipped away. One day he learned she had taken their child and moved back to her folks, and had died; she had always been sickly.

Years later — and he could hardly believe it had been that long — he heard the girl, Vera, was grown and married. He didn't know where she lived, and figured he didn't have any business trying to find out — it was too late to start acting like a father.

Nat's other big regret was the shooting — the worst thing that happened during his wild, senseless years. He and some other working cowhands had taken to stealing cattle for extra cash, and one day on a ranch over in New Mexico Territory they got caught using a running iron on some calves. The fight was on. While on the run from the ranch crew and firing back, Nat saw one of those chasing them was hit, and knew whose bullet had done it — he had turned in the saddle and fired, and immediately seen the rider go limp as a gunnysack and slide from the saddle.

Nat yanked his horse to a stop and spurred it back to the fallen cowboy. The other pursuers, by now, had scattered and pulled back.

"Damn, I'm sorry, pard!" Nat cried. "I didn't go to hit ya — we was just shootin' back, you know, to scare ya off," he heard himself say as he held the young man's head in the crook of his arm, his hand feeling the warm blood on the man's shirt. "Don't worry, I'll get ya to a doc!"

But the cowboy had gone pale, and Nat knew he didn't hear a word. Then came shooting again, and thundering hooves — the ranch crew was returning, and it sounded like with help. Nat jumped back on his mount and kicked it into a run.

A few days later, he heard the man was dead.

Nat had immediately changed his ways. He and the other rustlers weren't caught, and the shooting was finally forgotten — probably by everyone but him. Until that incident, using his six-shooter had been sport; he had never dreamed of harming anyone.

And after some forty years, he still told himself over and over that maybe, somehow, the poor cowboy knew he didn't mean it — that maybe he had a forgiving thought before he passed on.

One afternoon out on his porch, Nat's drowsing was shattered by hoots and hollers and gunshots. He jumped and nearly fell from the rope-bottom chair, but saw it was just two young scamps who had come in and bought a bottle a few hours earlier. They were still feeling their oats. Such activity in the middle of the day was rare, but happened occasionally when a cowpuncher or two with a few dollars between paydays snuck off from work to paint their tonsils.

One of these two he knew as a hand with a big cattle operation over in the next territory. All he knew about the other, a younger man who wore a black hat with a fancy silver band, was that he had a cocky manner about him Nat didn't care for.

"Hey, Nat, you sure do look peaceful in that old chair. Why doncha wake up and give us a drink on the house?" It was the one Nat knew. He and the other cowboy were galloping in a wide circle around the saloon, their six-shooters drawn and every now and then one of them firing into the air.

Nat knew how to handle such situations. If he paid them no mind, their liquor would soon wear off and they'd ride away.

But one of the riders yelled at the other, "Hey, ya wanna see me knock that chair out from under 'im? Watch me!" It was the younger one. His pistol roared — and lead dug into the porch flooring only a few yards from Nat's chair.

"Whoa, boys! That's enough of that!" Nat hollered. He thought about trying to hobble inside, but knew his bad leg wouldn't let him make it in time.

In moments the two were coming around again, and then came another shot, this one from the other rider, the slug hitting one of the rocks that supported the little shack, and whining off into nowhere.

At the same time, the younger rider raised his pistol in the air, as if thumbing back the hammer.

Nat felt the pain knife into his stomach an instant before he heard the blast. He immediately felt sick, then felt the chair wobble and tilt, and he fell to the floor.

Nat heard himself raving as he was loaded onto a buckboard and covered with one of the old blankets from his cot in the back room of the saloon. Burning throbs made him twist and curl like a worm on a hot rock as two men tried to keep him still.

"I'll get 'im! I can still ride and still handle a six-shooter, and I'll get 'im — that young one with the fancy hat. As soon as I get patched up, and quit hurtin', I'll get 'im!"

But even as he yelled, he knew that wouldn't be soon.

He closed his eyes and gritted his teeth against the anguish in his belly.

Nat looked at the people around him. He must have slept for days — though off and on. He'd been lifted and moved about, made to swallow awful-tasting medicine, and disturbed by crazy, feverish dreams, and the rising and falling of pain and feelings of sickness.

He reasoned he was in the town of Kenton and in the home of the doctor, who stood next to his bed. Also there were the doctor's wife; two lawmen, the one who was the local representative of this territory, plus another from over in New Mexico; and a minister. He knew them all, even the preacher.

Contemporary historical marker of No Man's Land.

Thunder in the Heartland

It was then that Nat knew he was dying – but also realized he wasn't particularly distressed.

"We want you to know, Nathan," the lawman from New Mexico said, "we're gonna get that hombre that shot you — both him and the one that was with 'im. We know who they are, and we'll have 'em both in jail by noon tomorrow."

Nat had to say what was on his mind, and say it now.

"I wanna tell ya somethin'," he said, gritting his teeth with every stab of pain. "I'm hurtin' a lot worse than when I fell on the Mesa and busted my leg, but ...   But them boys didn't mean no harm. I know they didn't shoot me a purpose. They was ... Well, they was just havin' a little sport. And I ain't mad at either one of 'em."

He could have said more, but knew nobody else would understand: The young man who shot him would be saddled with guilt for the rest of his life — which was a worse punishment than many folks could imagine. And once he knew that Nat had forgiven him, it would ease his load some.

It came to Nat that since he felt that way now, someone like him felt the same way a long time ago. He thought of the young cowboy dying in his arms.

Maybe, Nat figured, the fool-headed boy who shot him would someday have the kind of feelings he had now. And maybe it would be sooner than forty years.

"Now listen here, Nathan," the lawman said. "That hombre broke the law, and we're gonna get 'im. You gave us a good description, and we know 'im — he works for a cow outfit up in Colorado. We'll get 'im, and he might even hang after you ...   What I mean to say, if you don't get better ...."

With some effort, Nat raised his hand. "Whoa, I don't remember describin' nobody — I was hurtin' bad and musta been talkin' out of my head. I don't know who shot me. In fact, I never got a good look at either one of them galoots."

Nat suddenly felt better — in a way, even better than

---

he had in a long time. Then he relaxed and sank into a peaceful sleep.

When Nat opened his eyes, he thought he was dreaming. He was still in bed in the doctor's house, but standing over him was a woman, neat and pretty and maybe in her thirties. She was the only one in the room with him now. And there was something about her . . . .

It was Vera, his daughter! He was certain.

"Daddy!" she said, and swallowed. Her words came in a rush. "I guess I can call you that — I've wanted to call you that ever since I can remember. There's so much to say, I . . . I've always known where you were, Daddy, but could never decide if I should come to see you or not, after all these years . . . Well, especially since I felt like you didn't want to see me, and . . . ."

She paused and took a deep breath. "But then I learned you were hurt – I read about it in the Denver newspaper. Then I discovered that Jeff . . . Well, then I came as quickly as I could."

She bit her lower lip, and tears filled her large eyes. "Daddy, about this terrible thing that happened to you — I don't know quite how to say it. I'm just so very, very sorry, Daddy!" She wept loudly, as a small girl might.

It was Nat's time to speak. "Vera, honey, I don't understand just what you're talkin' about, but you ain't got nothin' to be sorry for. I'm the one to be sorry — all them years I meant to come back, and didn't. You don't know how much I wish I had. And, honey, about me gettin' shot, it ain't nothin' for you to worry about. It was just some crazy accident. It . ."

She had stopped crying, but her voice quivered. "Oh, Daddy, you just don't know! I guess you wouldn't know. You see, *my* marriage didn't go well, either. And you probably didn't know, Daddy, but I have a son, Jefferson, and I've had to raise him all by myself, and try to bring him up right — and I'm afraid I haven't done well at it."

She took another deep breath. "He's a good boy, but he's always been a little wild. The past few months he's been working south of the part of Colorado where we live and not far from here, and he . . . Oh, Daddy, he's . . . He's the one who shot you!"

"What? You mean I'm a grandpaw? I never thought about that possibility" — then his mood saddened. "'Course, I never thought that much about you at all, I guess."

She seemed shocked by his response. "Oh, Daddy, you still don't understand — and I know, it's so terrible it's hard to believe! My son, Jeff, he shot you — I know he didn't intend to, Daddy, and he didn't have any idea who you were, of course, but he shot you!"

She was crying again, her face in her hands. Her shoulders shook with the sobs. "Daddy, I know he'll have to go to prison, or somehow face what he's done, but the important thing is — Daddy, can you ever find it in your heart to forgive him?"

The room was warm, and quiet. Nat's pain returned and he fought it for a moment, and thought about what he would say.

"No, *you* don't understand, honey. I've already done that. I forgave him, and it didn't matter who he was. And I'm proud I did, but . . . But I'm a lot prouder of it *now*."

He closed his eyes briefly, but continued. "I don't want him to carry the kind of load I did. You tell that boy . . .. You tell Jeff I've forgiven 'im."

She looked at him, as if searching for the full meaning in his words. Both were silent for a moment.

Nat looked away from her and toward the window. The afternoon sun now came in and shone on the far wall. "I'm sorry, Vera, that I don't have nothin' to leave ya. I told the doc he could sell the saloon, to pay for his trouble, and to have me put up on the hill — there's a nice little spot there on the east side of a big mesquite."

Vera muffled a sob with her kerchief. "Oh, Daddy, all I ever wanted was to know you — to see you again someday. And I'm so thankful we finally found each other, even under such circumstances. It's strange, isn't it? If this terrible thing hadn't happened, I guess I never would have come."

Nat's body seemed to have less feeling, and he could tell it was going to be harder to get his words out, but he suddenly had more to say to his daughter.

"That's right, honey, and that's another reason I'm proud that it happened."

Vera looked puzzled, but wiped her eyes and listened intently as he went on.

"I wanna tell ya somethin' that might help you and that boy both have a happier life from here on out. For what it's worth to ya, I'm a contented man. Ya see, for years I've been saddled with two mighty heavy worries — and now, all because of that shootin' at the saloon, I don't have either one of 'em. And I feel better now than I've felt in a long, long time."

She had a look in her eyes like she understood – or at least was beginning to. She took her father's hand and pressed it to her face.

He smiled at her. "Sure is funny how things turn out, ain't it?"

That's when he closed his eyes. And he imagined he saw the sun lowering behind the saloon, and an eagle making circles over Black Mesa.

The Corner Saloon was possibly the meanest, vilest spot in present-day Oklahoma. Among other things, it was linked with a murder, which in turn resulted in the 1909 lynching of four men, including notorious Texas hired killer Jim Miller, in an Ada livery barn. This story, with a pre-statehood setting, was written with that dirty little drinking establishment in mind.

A Violent Streak

Sadness numbed Henry to the howling cold as he urged his horse over the frozen trail, aware of the revolver in the pocket of his mackinaw. He could almost hear Jason riding beside him. And if only he were, for now Henry needed his beloved kid brother more than ever, odd though the situation was. It was Jason's killer he was going after.

Henry had virtually raised Jason after their mother died several years ago. Before that, their father, always quick to rise to a challenge, had died in a shoot-out following a land dispute. After Henry married, Jason lived with them as the two brothers farmed and ran cattle on their inherited land. Henry and Lillian had no children, and Jason, some ten years younger than Henry, became like their son.

But while he and Jason had been close, they were different. At times Henry had wished he had Jason's nerve — although more often he considered his brother reckless, especially when he took him along when serving as a part-time lawman, a position Henry had reluctantly accepted after the regular constable died. Jason was always too eager for action, with fists or guns.

Then a few days ago, Jason had taken off alone to investigate a beating and robbery at the Border Saloon, refusing to wait till his older brother finished pulling a cow out of an icy creek. The place, on the bank of the Canadian River and at the edge of Indian Territory, was a hangout for whiskey smugglers and cutthroats.

"Don't worry, Hank, I'll handle it!" Jason had said, grinning as he swung into the saddle.

Henry left soon, but was slowed by the winter storm, and learned from another traveler that a ferry operator had fished Jason's body out of the river, a few miles downstream from the saloon. He had been shot in the back.

He returned and wired a U.S. deputy marshal at Tecumseh, but was told the deputy couldn't come right away — so he headed for the saloon alone.

Early that morning in the kitchen, Lillian had stood twisting her apron and pleaded as he wolfed down breakfast and gulped his coffee. He had already gone out into the cold darkness and fed and brushed Chief. He'd left the big roan waiting, saddled, in the barn.

Henry, don't go! At least, wait on the deputy," she said, agony in her voice. "That job you took has worried me sick. You're not gettin' any younger, and it's aged you something awful already. And now this!"

"You don't understand, Lil. Jason would roll in his grave if he knew I didn't go after his killers. You see, I owe it to his memory."

He rose and kissed her cheek, knowing he was trying too hard to seem matter-of-fact. "Now, if you need anything before I get back, go over to Doc Bradley's." The old doctor was not only their nearest neighbor, but, since they both had been blessed with good health, was less of a physician to them than their longtime, dearest friend.

It was like she hadn't heard him. "You know I loved

Jason, too, but I've said many a time I'm thankful you took your mother's even-tempered ways, instead of your daddy's. Jason was like him. He had that streak — a taste for violence. And it doesn't make sense for you to be like that, too. Not now." Her voice broke. "If . . . If I have to bury you, too, I won't be able to bear it!"

Trying to ignore her last words, he had buttoned up his coat. Outside, the wind whistled. "Lil, the boy was fool-headed, but he done what he thought was right. And if it was the other way around right now, I know what *he'd* do."

Henry stepped into the smoky warmth and dim lamplight, feeling the stares of at least half a dozen men. Then it hit him — as squarely as the odors of cheap liquor and squalid surroundings. Lillian was right. He had no business being here, and probably wouldn't leave alive.

Nervousness made him shudder as much as the cold he had just come in from. He moved to the bar, not sure what his next move would be — but keeping his right hand in his mackinaw pocket.

A burly, whiskered man in a grimy shirt appeared behind the bar. "We know why you're here, mister — and we don't know nothin' about that young feller gettin' killed. Now, what ya drinkin'?"

Henry heard chuckles behind him, and in the dingy mirror could make out the faces and smug grins.

In that instant, his face flashed hot, and his jaws tightened. By actually being here, he saw it all happen. His brother. Shot in the back!

He saw a quick movement in the mirror – but Jason was beside him. And he knew exactly what he was going to do. He pulled out the pistol and wheeled.

Let's get 'em, Jason! He thumbed back the hammer and fired. The small room lit up with explosions. Pain stabbed into the back of his left shoulder – at least one of the shots came from behind the bar. But he kept firing the pistol in his right hand, determined to take as many with him as he could.

"You're hurt, Henry, but you'll mend. You can't do much work for a spell, though. And no more part-time law work — not ever!"

Henry recognized the voice as Doc Bradley's as his mind began to clear. He was bandaged tightly and wrapped in a blanket, and was being loaded into a buggy.

The doctor explained that Lillian had roused him by beating on his door, so he hitched up his rig and headed for the saloon — and soon was passed by the U.S. deputy, his horse kicking up snow as he rode hell for leather.

He said that when he arrived at the saloon, shortly after the lawman had, it was all over. Of the saloon bunch, two were dead and three wounded, and in custody after being tended to by the doctor. A few others had fled, to parts unknown.

"To tell the truth, I doubted either one of us would get here on time," the doctor said, then hesitated.

"Henry, I know how you felt about Jason. But you've got to remember, the living go on living. Besides, you and Lillian are both healthy, and if you slow down and have a peaceful life . . . Well, you never know, of course, but sometimes couples older than you have younguns."

He frowned. "One thing bothers me. The deputy here said he didn't do much more than ride up with his gun and his badge — said you had almost cleaned out this whole rat's nest all by yourself! That doesn't sound like you, Henry. Did you do that?"

Henry barely smiled, but closed his eyes. "No. It wasn't me that done it."

It's doubtful Frank "Pistol Pete" Eaton, the mustachioed, legendary icon of Old West heroism who is enshrined in the emblems of Oklahoma State University, New Mexico State University and the University of Wyoming — or anyone slightly like him — was in the Harper County town of Salt Springs one day in 1921 when a horse race was interrupted by a bank robbery. But then, who can say?

Good with a Gun

Francis Easterling wasn't as quick as he'd once been, and his aim wasn't as keen. He was tired, too. So he was glad today was going to be his last "gunplay." That was how people described his fancy shooting, even if he had never shot a living thing, and never wanted to.

He smiled to himself as he strode through the small gathering in town for Trade Day, occasionally tipping his hat and greeting someone. His act always impressed people – it used to, anyway — partly because of his reputation. As always, they could believe what they wanted. And, as always – but for the final time – he'd give them a good show.

The place was one long, rough dirt street running from the Buffalo Northwestern Railroad's cattle-loading pen, a grain elevator and a bank at one end, to a livery barn and combination blacksmith shop and automobile garage at the other. In between were a small hotel, a lumberyard and a few stores. In the middle of it all was the town pump, and nearby in a vacant lot, a huge elm, the town's only shade tree.

Francis was even tired of his formal getup of silk vest, frock coat, string tie and huge felt hat, along with the two heavy pistols, especially on such warm days. It wasn't yet nine o'clock, and already he was sweating.

Other people felt the heat, too. Only a few cars were parked, and one team and wagon and maybe half a dozen saddle horses tied here and there. Also, the horse race segment of the celebration was scheduled for two hours later, and only about eight contestants had showed up.

And small wonder. The day before, Francis had driven his old flivver from Woodward, and noticed only one water hole within the some twenty-five miles. For some horseman, just getting here wasn't worth it.

Two riders were just pulling in, raising dust on the street as they walked their horses toward the town pump. Francis recognized one as Bud Pippin, a husky, boisterous type he had run into a few times before. Pippin usually only drank and became offensive, but Francis had him pegged as a troublemaker of some kind. The man with him was smaller, but a hard-looking cuss.

After the two sloshed their faces and refilled their canteens at the pump as their horses drank from the trough, they led their animals over to the shade tree. There, they pulled off their saddles, along with the attached saddlebags, slickers and canteens, and piled them on the ground where some others were. Some racers often did this to ease their horses' loads, and would race bareback, especially in warm weather.

Francis glanced to the other side of the street, where a few people strolled along the covered boardwalk in front of the local mercantile and a drug store. That's when he saw her — a mature but fetching woman, looking fresh as a daisy even in the heat. And immediately something about her made his heart skip a beat.

"Mary Jo! Is that you?" He almost shouted.

It *was* her! Mary Jo Shannon — at least, that used to be her name. She was the first girl he'd been sweet on, and the one he often wished he had married. They had drifted apart, and both had married, but over the years – after both had lost their spouses to early deaths — had exchanged a few letters, as dear friends.

Her eyes – the same pretty green they always were – lit up, and she hurried to him. They stood for a moment, ex-

Frank Eaton, the real "Pistol Pete." Copyright 1958, The Oklahoma Publishing Company.

changing blushing grins, then embraced in brother-and-sister fashion — which nevertheless thrilled Francis as much as the first time he hugged her, before either of them was twenty.

"Francis!" she said. "I never *dreamed* I would run into you today. I came out to Buffalo to see my sister, and heard about the to-do in this town and . . . ."

"And it's a wonder we both wound up here," he said. "They asked me to come and put on my act, and I didn't want to at first but finally agreed. If I'd known you'd be here, I'd have come if I had to walk — even in this heat!"

"Francis, you rascal! You haven't changed a bit." She gave him a playful slap on the chest and laughed. And the sound, as always, was pure music.

His wife, Ellen, had been a wonderful woman, and he had been true to her, despite his clinging memories of Mary Jo. When Ellen died nearly fifteen years ago, he continued to farm and run a few cows, but also took up his unusual avocation. As a boy, he had learned to shoot, becoming handy with a pistol. After his wife's death, he began touring as a sharpshooter. It was a good pastime.

He and Mary Jo brought each other up to date on things. He told her about this being his last shooting act.

"I'm plumb tired – gettin' old, I guess," he said, smiling. "Besides, I guess my time has passed. Seems like most people aren't interested in Old West attractions like me anymore. Now that the Great War's over, they think more about drivin' fast cars, and since this 'Prohibition' was passed, drinkin' all the bootleg whiskey they can get, and dancin' the Charleston."

"Oh? How do you know those things? Do you do all that?"

They both laughed. Francis had forgotten the happiness he'd felt just being near her.

"Mary Jo, tell you what – soon as this little shindig is over, let me treat you to dinner. I'll meet you at your sister's house over in Buffalo and . . . ."

Thunder in the Heartland

Bud Pippin walked up. If Francis had been the type, he'd have shot him then and there.

"Well, if it ain't Two-Gun Gus!" Pippin grinned in his usual disgusting way, and his loud voice drew onlookers. "I've heard all the stories about you, old man — how you was a deputy for 'Hanging Judge' Parker over at Fort Smith, killed a bunch of badmen, drove cattle up the Chisholm, used to ride with Charles Goodnight in Texas, fought wild Indians, and even danced with Belle Starr."

He stepped closer, his large frame only inches away and his breath, strong with liquor, in Francis' face. "And I've heard about how good you are with a gun – but I've also heard you don't have the guts to shoot nothin'. I bet you can't even . . . ."

Could be you're right, Pippin. But I'm here to put on a little show, then have a good time. So why don't you do the same?" Francis made himself smile, hoping it didn't show that his face had colored. He took Mary Jo by the arm and moved away.

Since boyhood, Francis had practiced so much his right hand felt empty without a gun in it. He had known the swollen thumb, aching hand and wrist, and days of frustration of miss after miss until finally becoming an expert — some would say a "gunman," "fast gun," even "gunslinger."

Yet, he had never so much as shot a jackrabbit – and never wanted to. He loved to shoot, but didn't cotton to the idea of killing things – even if he didn't correct the wild stories about himself. They didn't hurt his popularity at events like this one.

Now, though, he was hoping his reputation didn't blow up in his own face. Some no-account trifler like Hank Pippin might try to show off and push him into doing something that went against his grain.

Or, since he now wasn't sure about his ability, something worse could happen. If his aim was off, or if he hesitated a split second too long . . . .

"Time for the show, folks!" the man who headed up the Trade Day celebration sang out from a makeshift stage, a hay frame that had been rolled in front of the lumberyard. A decent gathering of people stood looking up, most of them in the shade of the elm. "Gather around, but stand back at a safe distance. Most of you have heard of Two-Gun Gus – he's gonna do some of his fancy shootin'."

Francis climbed onto the wagon and went through his act, firing his pistols – each of them a twenty-two on a forty-five Colt Peacemaker frame, as he considered the small caliber fairly safe in a crowd — hitting several small targets; and even using a mirror and firing backwards over his shoulder to burst balloons at an impressive distance.

After the clatter of applause, he gracefully thanked the crowd and announced this was his last show. He ceremoniously took off his two shiny revolvers, saying he would hang them up for good.

"Not yet, Two-Gun!" said the man who had presented him. "We want you to do one more thing: Fire the shot to start the horse race."

Francis agreed, but made a point in telling the crowd this would be his very final shot. With a flourish, he loaded only one of the pistols, with only one round. The spectators cheered and clapped, even though most of them couldn't even see the tiny twenty-two cartridge.

As the horses were in place, snorting and stamping with the same nervous excitement of their riders, Francis didn't see Pippin, or his hard-looking partner, either. Maybe they'd gotten drunk and were asleep in the shade somewhere.

"Ready . . . May the best horse win!" the man yelled, and nodded at Francis, who pointed the pistol into the clear blue sky – and was tightening his finger on the trigger when someone yelled with alarm.

"The bank's been robbed! The bank's been robbed!" A man in a bloody white shirt – apparently the banker himself – was coming toward them in an open-top Model T, screaming and trying to keep the car in the ruts of the dirt street.

A second later, something drew Francis' eyes to a place just outside the shade of the elm where he saw Mary Jo, her face pale with fright, and behind her, Pippin, his right arm locked around her neck. In his left hand, he held his horse's reins.

"Don't noboby move – especially you, Easterling! And drop that pistol! I ain't got a gun, but I can sure give this old lady a sore neck. You boys can have this race as soon as we're gone — but you better go in another direction. We're takin' this woman with us, and if anybody follows us, she ain't gonna come back."

Pippin's partner came loping up, jumped off his horse, and with a long pistol shooed back the banker, who was wobbling as he tried to get out of his car. He obviously had been clubbed by the same pistol during the holdup.

"Saddle my horse!" Pippin, still holding Mary Jo in a choking grip, yelled to his partner. "Don't take time for your saddle – I gotta ride double with her, so I need mine. And put the money in my saddlebags."

His eyes shot back to Francis. "And I said drop that gun, Easterling! He tightened his hold on Mary Jo's neck, and Francis heard a soft whimper. His face stung with hatred.

But something seemed to dawn on Pippin, because he grinned. "You only got one shot anyhow, Two-Gun, and that little twenty-two ain't much good against this forty-four we're packin'." He glanced at his cohort, who was still holding the pistol while moving toward Pippin's saddle.

"Besides," he said, plainly enjoying himself, "I don't think you'll take a chance on hittin' her, even if you are as good a shot as they say you are."

Francis wiped sweat out of his eyes. He had to keep calm and think fast. He had always imagined it might be his own life on the line someday, but never dreamed it would be Mary Jo's.

For once in his life, he could shoot someone without the slightest qualm. But which one? If he put a slug in

Pippin's forehead, he'd have an empty gun against the partner's forty-four. And if he shot the partner . . . .

He removed his hat, holding it up and shielding his eyes from the sun as he studied the whole scene before him.

"Well, what ya waitin' on, *Two-Gun?*" Pippin said. His grin was more menacing. "Either use that pistol or put it down. But I'd make up my mind pretty quick."

Francis moved. Just as Pippin's partner was about to pick up the saddle, and as fast as a gust of prairie wind, he fired.

Surprise popped on all faces. Especially Pippin's – but only until he realized the shot apparently did no harm, the shooter having missed on purpose. His face twisted into one of his mean grins. "Just like I figured, old man. You don't have the guts to shoot nobody!"

After his horse was hurriedly saddled, Pippin swung Mary Jo onto his mount, and climbed up behind her, and he and his cohort kicked the horses into a gallop, heading south. In seconds they were over the rise and lost in the sage.

Francis stood on the stage and wilted, filled with worry and guilt. He had let them take Mary Jo – even if he had taken the only choice he could.

"He missed!" one man in the crowd said, sounding like he couldn't believe his own words.

Francis could barely hear one of the other spectators say, "Guess you can't expect anything else from a carnival sharpshooter."

Francis owed some explanation, so, making himself sound calm, offered one: "I think it's best this way. Not everything can be solved by shooting people."

A few of them nodded, but didn't say anything. And they all looked like they were youngsters who had just been told their dime novel hero was a faker.

In less than an hour, the sheriff, Rufus Willoughby, pulled up in a Model T, overloaded with his large body and four deputies.

"I've thought this all out," Willoughby said. "They gotta

be headin' for Woodward, plannin' to catch the passenger train there. Now, between us and the sheriff down in that county, we'll get 'em sooner or later. But the sooner the better, since they got a hostage with 'em."

He unfolded a map, and explained that the robbers, being horseback, surely had taken the shortest route, which was rough, so they couldn't be followed by automobile. There was no water along that way, but a full canteen would get them to Woodward.

"So here's what we gotta do: A couple of my deputies, and any of you boys that wanna go, will take out after 'em on some of these horses. You'll have to ride hard to catch 'em, but make sure you do – if that lady dies in the heat, it's gonna look bad for my office. Now get goin'!"

Francis knew it was time to speak up. "Sheriff, there's an easier way to get 'em."

Willoughby stared at him, hard. "Oh? Is that a fact? I heard about how hard you tried to stop 'em from leavin'. Mind tellin' me about this easy way to catch 'em?"

"Well, we'll go by car, and take the longest route, by road. Then we'll wait on 'em at the water hole."

The sheriff's wide face reddened. "I just got done explainin' all that! Why would they go to the water hole?"

"Well, right about now Pippin's discovered that his canteen has a hole in it, right down close to the bottom. So they'll change course."

"What? How in the devil would you know that? Besides, any fool would notice right off if his canteen had a hole in it."

"Well, not right off, especially when somebody else had saddled his horse and they were in a hurry. Not only that, but a twenty-two makes a neat, tiny little hole."

Willoughby still looked puzzled, and even more so when the handful of spectators began cheering and laughing.

Francis headed for his flivver. It didn't go as fast as some cars, but he still planned on being the first one there. He

---

could hardly wait to see Mary Jo, and he bet she'd take him up on dinner.

This story alludes to the state's reputation during the early 1930s as a hotbed for criminals such as "Pretty Boy" Floyd, and is further inspired by a personal boyhood experience of the author. It was first published in the September 1999 issue of ByLine *magazine. It has since undergone a few changes.*

Another Dry Fall

Me and Millie were taking a Sunday afternoon drive out east of town, and, like always, I thought of the old cellar. But this time I couldn't shake off the memory. It was like it all happened yesterday. We were having a dry fall, with pastures thin and buzzing with grasshoppers, the sumac bushes, usually red by now, as gray and dirty as the cotton fields, and the scraggly blackjack trees even uglier than normal — the way it was that time around Okfuskee Switch.

Millie gets tired of hearing my boyhood stories and tells me I should think about things in the present — the grandkids, for instance. Why, I hadn't taken little Timmy Dale fishing in months! But when I pulled over and stopped about where I remembered we used to pull the fence wires down and lead the horses across, Millie just slumped back and sighed. I guess she knew I was going to tell it anyway.

It all started when me and Tom Webster and little Gordy Ellison, who followed us around, discovered the old caved-in storm cellar one day when rabbit hunting on the Mathis place, and decided to make a hideout. We cleaned it out, laid limbs across the top and covered them with dirt, and fixed it up right smart.

"Boy Howdy! This is neat!" I said when we were sitting inside, the lantern lit and a little fire in the stove we had made from a lard can and a piece of rusty stovepipe.

"Remember now," Tom said, "we ain't tellin' *nobody* about this place. And when we're here we'll keep a small blaze goin', that won't hardly smoke, so old man Mathis won't see it."

"Dang right!" I said. "And when we leave we'll cover the door real good with brush."

And Gordy said, "Dang right! Boy Howdy!"

It *was* neat too.

We'd run in and out, playing outlaws like Bill Doolin, the Dalton brothers and Jesse James. We figured they probably came right through here at one time or another, maybe even holed up in this same old cellar.

But most of the time we'd just sit inside and talk about Zane Grey stories and Dick Tracy in the funny papers, and tell scary tales and jokes we'd heard from the men who loafed around downtown. And with the dim light flickering on the walls of dirt and crumbly concrete, it was all fascinating stuff.

We carried water up from Snake Creek — it wasn't running, but wasn't plumb dry either — to make coffee. We had brought a can and three Garrett snuff glasses. And when we managed to sneak a sack of tobacco and cigarette papers, the Bull Durham smoke, burning wood, coffee and kerosene all made for the most wondrous smell imaginable.

Me and Tom did about all the talking, since Gordy was younger than us and, as everybody knew, wasn't quite right. I never knew his real first name. People called him that because his head was round like a gourd. But he was happy. He'd just sit and listen and grin, as they say, like a possum eating persimmons.

We decorated the place by hanging our weapons on the wall. Besides our bean flips — some people call them "slingshots" — Tom had a hunting knife and I had part of a frog gig. But Gordy had the neatest thing: a real pistol — a Smith & Wesson thirty-two caliber, five-shot revolver, nickel-plated with a pearl handle, that he had found someplace. It wouldn't shoot. The firing pin was gone, the ejector broken, and it was corroded some and the handle cracked. But to Gordy it was still a real gun, and a beautiful thing, sure enough.

Sometimes me and Tom also talked about the girls in school, and how they looked in their basketball suits — although I never mentioned the one girl I *wanted* to talk about, since my ears stung when other fellas did. That was Jennie Lou Akins, who I stared at in class a lot — but who never looked back at me.

About this part of the story, Millie laughed. She hadn't known me then. I met Millie at a pie supper over in another county and we've been married for thirty-something years.

Anyway, while me and Tom talked, Gordy would take his pistol down and polish it on his overalls, then hang it back up and sit and look at it, and grin.

That old cellar was our special place on weekends and after school for well into winter. On Saturdays and Sundays we'd get up before the roosters crowed and rush through our chores and be there early. We'd ride out from town — me and Tom had horses, and Gordy rode behind one of us. We'd take the horses through right about at this spot where the old fence sagged, and stake them out in the woods.

Mr. Mathis didn't mind people on his land if they didn't start any fires — we didn't plan on him knowing about our stove and us smoking, of course. And his two nearly grown sons, both smart alecks, were lazy and seldom got out on the place.

So we figured our hideout was safe and we left most of our stuff there between visits. We made Gordy leave his pistol, too, especially since he had to carry it in his back pocket when he was hanging on behind one of us, and it was bound to fall out when the horses were in a lope.

We never dreamed that outsiders would find the place — especially real outlaws. And that soon the whole community would know about it, and we'd be famous.

It happened one bright, cold Saturday morning when somebody thundered on the door. We hushed, and sat like scared rabbits.

"Must be old man Mathis — he musta heard the horses," Tom whispered. "Heck, I knew I shouldn't have brought that mare out here while she's horsein'!"

We had heard his mare whinny a few times, but knowing she was in heat and got feisty when another horse came down the road, hadn't paid much attention.

Then the door swung open.

It sure wasn't Mr. Mathis! The man was husky, and in one hand he had a pistol — a big automatic type like Dick Tracy used. Another man loomed behind him.

I just knew we were goners. Gordy started to snatch his pistol off the wall — I guess to hide it — but Tom grabbed his arm. Still, I wet my pants.

Well, believe it or not, it was Rex Carlisle and one of his gang, known throughout eastern Oklahoma as a bad bunch. We didn't know their names then, though it was plain they weren't Sunday school teachers.

Turns out they had robbed a bank somewhere the day before and at night turned off the highway at Okfuskee Switch to head east toward their hideout in the Cookson Hills. Their Model A ran out of gas halfway up the hill. I guess a wagon and team came by after daylight and they heard Tom's mare cutting up, and then found the cellar.

"I'll be damned! Just some kids," the husky man said.

"What we gonna do with 'em, Rex?" the other said.

"Well, we can't let 'em go tellin' people they seen us, so we sure gotta do *somethin'* with 'em."

They hog-tied Tom and left him there and pulled me and Gordy up behind them on the horses — I guess this was their best plan at the moment. They couldn't take all three of us, and Tom was the heaviest.

Thunder in the Heartland

Whatever their intentions, I was wishing now that our hideout wasn't such a good one. I figured nobody would find Tom before the fire died out and he froze, and gosh knows what would happen to me and Gordy.

Also, it hit me that nobody would miss us right away. Me and Tom stayed all night with one another so often that my folks would think I was at his house and his folks would think he was at mine. Gordy lived with his mother and a bunch of brothers and sisters in a shack down by the cotton gin. She took in washing and sold choc — you know, home-made beer, named after the Choctaws — and everybody knew she was too busy to count the kids every night.

The outlaws kept off the roads. They whipped the horses up and headed east across the Mathis place, weaving through the blackjacks at a full gallop. I suddenly remembered that when they dragged us out of the cellar I hadn't seen Gordy's thirty-two on the wall. Then I looked over at Gordy hanging on behind Rex Carlisle and saw it in Gordy's back pocket — just as it was falling out.

I prayed the outlaws wouldn't see it.

And they didn't — and probably wouldn't have if that crazy little Gordy hadn't turned loose and jumped backwards off the horse. I guess he'd rather be killed than lose that old pistol.

And he nearly was. He landed on his feet but, just like a hobo I saw jump off a moving freight train once, flipped over on his head.

Rex Carlisle cussed and both horses were jerked to a stop.

I shut my eyes.

Gordy wobbled to his feet. When I looked again, I was relieved to see that what was all over his face wasn't blood — he had rolled through a fresh cow pile. He stumbled around till he spotted his thirty-two, and snatched it up.

Rex Carlisle reached Gordy just as Gordy was polishing the pistol on his overalls, and Carlisle whipped out his big Dick Tracy automatic.

I shut my eyes again, and *sure enough* prayed this time.

But Rex Carlisle didn't shoot. I guess he figured the noise wasn't necessary — he just clubbed Gordy with his pistol. I'll never forget the sound it made.

Gordy looked awful — it *was* blood on his face this time — but he was still on his feet, and still holding his thirty-two.

Rex Carlisle snatched it out of his hand, broke it open, then smirked, and slung it way off into the brush.

Gordy looked puzzled. Then his face twisted up and he started crying. It was even a worst sight than when Rex Carlisle clubbed him.

When we came to a fence, the outlaws cut it and we crossed the road. They cut the other fence and we went across an open pasture, then finally headed down into Big Muddy Bottom.

It was nearing sundown. I couldn't help but wonder if me and Tom and Gordy would see the next day.

We didn't know it then, but Tom was already safe, and a sheriff's posse, packing pistols, rifles and shotguns, was waiting up ahead. Mr. Mathis had got to the cellar shortly after we left and discovered Tom — guess he'd heard Tom's mare cutting up, too. They high-tailed it to Mr. Mathis' house and he rang up Cletus Hales, the local deputy.

Cletus Hales was skinny as a rail fence and had a whining little voice that made people laugh, except people who knew him.

And they knew he was nobody to trifle with. It was said he was part Indian, and could smell a whiskey still for miles and was like a coon dog at picking up a trail — animal's or man's. He was meaner than a biting sow and could fight like a badger, and he never missed with his Colt thirty-eight six-shooter.

He studied the tracks, then rang up the sheriff in Muskogee and announced where he was aiming to head off the outlaws. The sheriff could meet him there if he wanted to.

So, just as dark was coming on and I was shivering and so scared I was about to puke, we rode out of some woods and into a patch of ragged cotton — and all at once in the cold, still air I heard a whole bunch of hammers click.

The outlaws didn't pay any heed to that whining little command to throw up their hands, so when Cletus Hales yelled again it was to warn me and Gordy.

But we both already were jumping backwards off the horses — a second before all hades broke loose. We skittered like lizards through the cotton stalks back to the woods, while above us it was like the Fourth of July.

Rex Carlisle's right arm was shot up — I'm sure by Cletus Hales' Colt — and his partner was out colder than a cucumber after Tom's mare bucked him off. The trees looked like there had been a hailstorm.

Cletus Hales easily persuaded Rex Carlisle to name the other gang members, who were then arrested in the Cookson Hills.

Me and Tom and our horses came through everything fine. And Gordy did, too, except for where Rex Carlisle clubbed him. The doctor said it would leave an ugly scar.

But Gordy didn't mind. When the Muskogee newspaper did a front-page story about how three boys, armed only with slingshots — we hadn't mentioned Gordy's thirty-two — helped capture the Rex Carlisle outlaw gang, the photographer made Gordy mind even less by saying the bandage on his head would make the picture more impressive.

The photograph showed all five of us, me and Tom holding our horses, with Gordy in the middle, facing the camera. Gordy sure was grinning.

Overnight, we were big shots.

Especially Gordy. At school during recess, boys kept offering him marbles and arrowheads and such to show them his scar — which Gordy was glad to do for nothing, until the bandage was so loose it came off for good.

In class when I glanced at Jennie Lou Akins, she was looking back and smiling. She slipped me a note saying she had some extra fried pies in her lunch box. When we ate together at noon, I was so excited I couldn't say anything, so kept my mouth full of fried pie.

Me and Tom told Gordy we'd help find his thirty-two when we went back to our hideout — which Mr. Mathis said we were certainly welcome to do. He even said we could go through his pasture gate instead of through the fence.

We couldn't find the pistol.   But Gordy, like us, was happy anyway about how things had worked out, overall.

Until, that is, we found we were *too* welcome at our hide-out — if you could still call it that. Mr. Mathis' two smart-aleck sons were there to meet us every time we rode up to the gate.

Then they would scrunch down into that little cellar with us — I guess Mr. Mathis didn't trust us not to start any more fires — and would sit there wisecracking and telling jokes, not funny jokes like ours, but nastier ones that didn't make sense. And they'd smoke — I guess it was okay for them — and their fancy Lucky Strike ready-rolls didn't smell nearly as good as our Bull Durham makings had.

But worst of all, with them there we didn't feel free to talk — about Zane Grey stories, girls, or anything else.

Finally, one evening after school we managed to sneak out there by ourselves.

But then a strange thing happened.

We first noticed that Gordy wasn't grinning. He acted sick. Then we figured out why, because we felt the same way.Our hideout was the same place it was before — but then, it *wasn't* the same. The little stove, the coffee fixings, the pegs on the wall for our weapons, all looked dinky to us now — the way we knew they looked to Mr. Mathis' sons, and would to anybody else.

When it was just us, there was something special about the place. Now, there wasn't.

That evening when we left, we didn't say anything, but took our stuff with us.

Later, at home doing my chores, I thought of a day in

December some years earlier when an older boy — Booger Red Mitchell, they called him — told me in his grinning, buck-toothed way that there was no Santa Claus. As soon as I'd turned away from him, I cried, but somehow felt a little older.

After that last day in the cellar, me and Tom didn't run around together much, and I guess Gordy started following somebody else around. I finally got tired of Jennie Lou Akins' fried pies, and started sparking other girls.

Gordy left when his mother got the chance to move with some man out to California. A little later, both me and Tom went off to the war, in different uniforms. Tom never came back.

When Mr. Mathis died, his sons sold their land to a man from Texas who raised Santa Gertrudis cattle, during a time when it was pretty and green up here and extra dry down there.

I later read in the Muskogee paper where Cletus Hales died. His age wasn't mentioned, but he must have been, as they say, older than dirt. And I heard Gordy had wandered out onto a busy four-lane in front of a semi. He probably didn't know what hit him; I sure hope that's the way he went.

Millie was quiet for a minute, then said, "You know, I'm sure I've heard that story before, though not all the details. I know you feel blue about your two friends, but we all have to bury the past sometime.

"And about your playhouse — well, kids shouldn't be playing in a nasty old cellar anyway."

Some things Millie just doesn't understand. I opened the car door and said I'd be right back.

I finally found it. Besides two rusty hinges and some pieces of crumbly-looking wood among the scattered dried chunks of cow manure, the only sign of a cellar was a slight depression. It looked like a sunk-in grave.

That's when it hit me: For years I had wanted to go back there, and now the yearning was gone. There were too many other places to go that I hadn't been. And so little time.

I thought of Millie waiting out by the road. Maybe I'd

surprise her and take her up to Muskogee for supper.

Before leaving, I kicked around in the dirt a little, looking for Gordy's thirty-two. But I didn't expect to find it, figuring by now it would be rusted to pieces.

Unless some boy came along and found it shortly after it was lost. Some boy like Timmy Dale.

Maybe that's what happened.

In Atoka County in 1934, following reports that a minister in a small community displayed an unwholesome interest in children, four men were charged with his savage mutilation, though not convicted. The principal vigilante, according to reliable confidants, finally decided the preacher was innocent, and became "a tortured man." While the following story is fictitious and isn't meant to chronicle the actual case, the two have similarities.

Rumors Heard in Heaven

Leo Morgan, who farmed and traded in livestock, was tall and solid and to those around him seemed ageless — he could be guessed as thirty-something, or a sturdy seventy — and in an overbearing way that was as much a part of him as his cold hazel eyes, commanded an easy respect.

That's why anyone in the community would say that no two human beings were more opposite than Leo and Silas Hamby, an elderly lay minister with one dress shirt and tie, and who was truly a gentle soul.

However, probably no one suspected that the two would come together in a monumental conflict.

Leo Morgan made up for a lack of grace with his blunt, imposing presence. He was insensitive to everything in life except the material elements necessary to support his family, plus satisfy his own urges and vanity. He owned a rattling flatbed truck, but on Saturdays came to town wearing big hat, high-topped boots and spurs and riding a powerful, wild-eyed gelding.

Silas Hamby had long been the pastor of the town's tiniest church — an obscure denomination with a lengthy name that many laughed at — and was best known because of jokes that his dull sermons put most of his small flock to sleep every Sunday. It was also said his summertime outdoor revivals rarely netted a convert.

Leo Morgan came from poor but decent people and a traditional rural Bible Belt upbringing. Also, he was staunchly fair in business, and displayed an almost rabid determination to pursue any course he decided was right.

But there was a meanness about him. At home he was harsh, holding a rigid control over his horses and wife and kids as well — any of them, when slightly balky in their respective roles, would feel his whip or the flat of his large hand. Elsewhere, other men stepped out of his way, avoided his hard, direct look, and laughed at anything he said that he considered witty.

And indeed Leo Morgan relished a challenge, especially in front of a crowd.

Like when, following a piddling disagreement at the cotton gin, he yanked off his jacket and thoroughly whipped Owen Sanders, the scale master — himself husky, but easygoing and not much of a hand to fight — then kept pounding until the young man was senseless.

"Don't ever tell *me* my load ain't what I say it is!" Leo, his eyes wide and flashing, swore between clenched teeth, obviously for the benefit of spectators — Owen Sanders was beyond hearing anything.

Silas Hamby never did anything to draw such attention.

And since his congregation was small, and since he had to travel afoot, he was recognized for what little he did accomplish by only a few people — even if those followers were indeed devoted.

"I'll never forget, back before Herman passed away," said an aged widow, "when he was losing his sight, Silas and Bonnie came over and brought their Bible and a pile of GRIT magazines, and they'd take turns readin' to 'im for hours. I'll declare, that preacher did Herman a world of good!"

"It made me feel bad that we had never set foot in his church, let alone donated anything to it," she added. "But it didn't matter to him whether we went to any church or not — he's a true man of God, that Silas is."

Others remembered one winter when Silas killed all his chickens to take to a large family plagued by the flu and a flooded hay crop.

And gradually, more residents were becoming aware of how every Christmas season Silas' meager collection plate proceeds went for goodies that he personally delivered to poor children. It was that custom — of which Silas was obviously quite proud — that started the scandal about child molestation, although the term wasn't common back then.

It so happened the talk, which created more excitement than local people had known in years, greatly aroused Leo Morgan. For the type of man he was, it seemed to fill a need.

It was one spring evening, when the rumors were ripe, that Leo and three other men were sharing a bottle in the town wagon yard. A short piece away was the home of Silas Hamby, where inside a small, neat yard surrounded by white blooming honeysuckles on a wire fence, soft light spilled through a screen door, along with the smells of supper cooking, and sounds from a radio — the unmistakable patter of jokes and laughter that typified "Fibber McGee and Molly."

While the dwelling was modest, the quiet, friendly setting bespoke a comfortable life that Leo perceived as both foreign and uppity, and it bolstered his decision.

One of the other men spoke, his eyes watery after a pull at the bottle. "Messin' with them little girls! Ain't that a damn shame?"

"And him a preacher, too!" said another, glancing up from rolling a Prince Albert cigarette.

Leo opened his pocketknife and spat on the steel tire of a wagon wheel, then put the blade to it and began stroking back and forth. He seldom smiled, but did now. "By God, I bet I can take his mind off that!"

The other men chuckled. But they were nervous sounds, as Leo's companions, though rough-hewn, lacked the iron resolve of the man they were about to follow.

The news spread like a grassfire. And the happening immediately became far more unforgettable than the scandal itself, and affected the community as nothing had before.

Some said the four men drove Silas Hamby to the woods just outside of town in a Model A Ford one of the railroad workers borrowed from his brother-in-law; others said Leo used his own flatbed truck.

Other speculated details flew in whispers, even into neighboring counties. And some accounts of the incident, particularly at first and among the male residents, were spread aloud, and were graphic and often accompanied by base humor.

"You hear what Leo said when one of the others got scared that the preacher might die?" said a downtown loafer, well experienced at telling the story. "Ol' Leo told 'im he'd cut many a hog and calf, and never had lost one yet!'"

Some giggled at the popular talk that "the 'evidence' was found hangin' on the thorn of a horse apple tree."

But the images conjured by even the most reliable and conservative reports could not have been more telling – a frail oldster dragged into the dark woods and his thin white legs held spraddled for the indelicate surgery, as his small, gray wife, left in the vehicle, sat trembling as she prayed.

Never in the community's history had there been anything so talked about, though often in hushed, horrified tones. Many people lamented that the name of their normally peaceful town would forever be stained by this vile outrage. Some of them wept.

Others said the preacher must have done what he was accused of — especially seeing how he didn't go to the sheriff — and justice, however rough, had been served.

Finally, a number of residents told themselves it never happened, that it was all gossip. Then they wished that were so.

Following a short stay in the hospital, Silas Hamby looked well enough — he gained weight, in fact, almost overnight losing his frail appearance, and his face took on an odd puffiness.

But he announced his retirement to the few people attending his next and final Sunday service, during which his talk dealt with the Gospel of Luke, 23rd chapter, and emphasized the words Jesus spoke from the cross.

He and Bonnie soon moved to another part of the state. It was said one of their children lived there.

It was a few years later, after the small frame building that had been Silas Hamby's church was used for storing feed and such and the lot fenced for a hog pen, that word was received of his death.

That's when the change in Leo Morgan began taking place — possibly because the preacher had died; or that word got out that the girl who raised the first allegations recanted her story; or simply because of the clarity of matters that often comes with time.

Leo started going to church — one of the town's larger ones that his family attended — and finally one night even joined others in going forward during the invitational hymn.

One of the regulars at the blacksmith shop voiced an astonishment that epitomized that of the whole community. "I never thought I'd see the day Leo Morgan would go up front and get saved at a revival meetin'." He grinned around a chew of tobacco. "It's hard to believe he'd get down and cry and sling snot and carry on like the rest of 'em. But from what I hear, that's just what he done!"

When Leo came to town, younger residents saw him as just another old man, bent with age and sickness, and who walked as if dragging a weight. They immediately were aware of his nervous, jerky movements and sad eyes, which never looked directly at anyone. Others who knew him before could scarcely believe he was the same man.

As Leo Morgan changed, so did the memory of the preacher whose name would always be voiced at the mention of his.

And because of it all, the happening would come to be considered, even among the community's more coarse population, something fateful and preordained.

Silas Hamby would be spoken of — during religious gatherings, in town and in the fields — in a manner usually reserved for saints. For it would be said he was the only mortal since the Crucifixion to make a true sacrifice — that he had suffered the ineffable to reclaim a lost soul, and had brought the devil to his knees.

This story is about tornadoes, as common in Oklahoma as red-tailed hawks – and how in the state's rural areas in the late 1930s, one might have changed a few lives.

Storm Season

Maggie sat in her aunt's living room during a meeting of the church ladies, very aware of her condition. Her red print dress, which her mother had made for her seventeenth birthday, was limp and wrinkled except where it stretched across her middle, and the white collar was dirty. She knew her nose must be sunburned and shiny. She tried to avoid looking at the others, sipping at the glass of ice tea and pretending to alternately study the Biblical painting on the fan she held in her lap, and one of the oval-framed pictures high on a wall.

That morning, after her mother tearfully packed her small valise, her father had driven her in his pickup to the highway and bought her bus ticket. Upon arriving, and after Maggie walked a good ways along the dirt streets from the general store, Aunt Lottie met her outside and hugged her the way she did when she was small, and explained she was hosting a Saturday afternoon social of her women's Bible class.

"It's awfully nice to have you with us, young lady," one of the women said.

Maggie looked back and tried to smile. The woman had a pinched face and thick glasses.

"When is the baby due?"

She mumbled something, hoping it would suffice for an answer.

"You're not from these parts, are you?" the woman said. "Maybe I'd know your husband's folks. What's your last name again?"

Maggie tried to think of what best to say. She glanced at her Aunt Lottie, who sat straight, her aged but kind eyes open wide and mirroring Maggie's own moment of dilemma. She swallowed as sweat trickled down between her breasts. The grandfather clock in the hall ticked away. She felt queasy, and needed to pee.

She looked about, hoping there was a bathroom, but recalled that when she arrived Aunt Lottie had given her a drink in a dipper from a bucket — the old house, though clean and neat, didn't have indoor plumbing.

Maggie excused herself, and as she started through the kitchen, Aunt Lottie called after her. "If you're going outside, honey, there's a parasol on the back porch. It's about to rain."

She stayed in the outhouse longer than necessary, thankful for the solitude. Presently, from outside came thunder and the clean smell of rain, and the first few large drops plopped on the little roof. Through the crack where the door, once painted white, was latched to the frame, she saw the day had darkened. Home seemed farther away than the thirty miles or so. Home, where she used to lie in bed at night and dream about someday meeting the perfect guy.

A few years ago, she had met Rusty – he insisted on being called his nickname instead of Clarence, and yelled at her when she occasionally called him his real name. Despite his cocky ways – other girls said he was "stuck on himself" — she wondered how she could ever live without him. If only she could've made him see that they were meant for each other. If only she could talk to him now. If her thoughts could somehow reach him. If only . . . .

She closed her eyes tightly, the way she used to when she hoped it would make her wishes come true.

She wondered briefly if she would ever see her family again. She would miss her mother, and especially little Tommy Dean. It was hard to imagine not watching her brother grow up. Someday she would probably see him, but he would be grown then.

The next burst of thunder seemed to split the sky, and with it came hard rain, then hail. It hammered on the roof, and then quickly ceased, leaving an eerie silence.

Maggie organized herself as best she could, wiping her eyes with her dress, and stepped outside. Maybe by now the women would be gone.

A great gust slammed the outhouse door behind her. The wind screamed and wrapped the red dress tight around her body. It pulled at the roots of her hair. Dirt stung her face as she stumbled toward the house, blinded by the dust. Her aunt was coming out the back door, carrying what appeared to be blankets and a water jug.

Once inside the cellar, they sat in the cozy lantern light. Aunt Lottie smiled and took her hand. "Don't be scared, honey. We're safe from the cyclone. And don't you worry — you have a home here as long as you want, and the baby, too. Your daddy's harsh, but he's a decent man."

"Thank you, Aunt Lottie. I don't want to trouble you any longer than I have to, though. I . . ." She tried to keep her voice from breaking. "I may just stay for a few days. I think Rusty . . . I mean, it may be that . . . ."

"Honey, I know it's hard for you to understand now, but the first man that comes along isn't always the right man. Besides, oftentimes things turn out for the best."

Maggie forced a smile. Her aunt meant well, but surely couldn't remember being young. Her mother had told her a little about Aunt Lottie. Her husband had left her soon after they married, then was accidentally killed in the oil fields. She raised a son, who moved away long ago, and she had lived on some kind of small pension, plus sometimes worked, caring for the sick and elderly. But Maggie couldn't imagine this woman ever having feelings, and problems, like hers.

Aunt Lottie seemed to have read her thoughts. "Mark my word, honey, life will go well if you do like I've done – be strong, do what you think is right, and then trust to Providence. And all told, I have lots to be thankful for."

She leaned closer and looked into Maggie's eyes. "And you're so young and pretty and kind-hearted, like your mother – I remember she was that way, even as a little girl. You deserve respect, but if you don't respect yourself, you won't get it from anybody else."

"But, Aunt Lottie, I . . . I *love* him. I . . . ."

"When you get right down to it, it's the same thing. Respect is what you young people call love. And if you start feeling that way about yourself now, sometime you'll look back on this day and smile, mark my word."

Maggie wished she *could* forget Rusty, and their times together – precious memories, except for the guilt and shame she had felt after the night he first coaxed her into the back seat of his daddy's car. And many times after that she disliked his cold manner. He could be so loving, so true; but immediately afterwards he acted like he barely knew her.

But what upset her even more was the difference in their beliefs, and how he scoffed about hers. They argued about this often, although this disturbed her far more than it did him.

"Rusty, I know this sounds silly to you, but this feeling I have about us keeps bothering me," she had said once after he stopped the car where they regularly parked. "To me, some things in life are *meant* to be, and sometimes I'm afraid we're *not* meant to be together. It's not only because we're different – I mean our families, our homes and all. It's just that – well, this feeling I have."

He had laughed, and pulled her closer. "Come on, let's

get out. We'll talk about it out on the blanket."

Their serious arguments had started after she told him she was pregnant. They could go someplace where nobody knew them and get married, she pleaded — and where he could also find a good-paying job, like Wichita, maybe even Dallas. But he had insisted he couldn't – his dad expected him to eventually work for him in his feed mill business. And until then, he liked his part-time farm work.

His work! This afternoon he would be in the hay field, and it must be storming there, too, since it wasn't that far away. He had been working with the haying crew for the past two weeks. At home, her family had their cellar, but Rusty would be in the open – with the winds, and the lightning! She closed her eyes and prayed.

When Aunt Lottie opened the cellar door, the back porch was nearly torn away and the chicken house was gone. A long piece of tin was wrapped around the well house. Neighboring houses were damaged also. But all was still. It was a strange picture of calamity and peace.

A delayed relief swept over Maggie. She and her aunt could be dead now, the cellar covered with tons of the storm's wreckage. She had been so deep into her problems, and her concern for Rusty, that the danger to herself — and her unborn child — hadn't occurred to her at the time.

Aunt Lottie beamed. "Look, honey! There's hardly any damage at all. With the help of friends, we'll have the place back to normal before you know it. And it's cleared off already, and this ought to be the last storm of the season."

It was just before sundown, and the gentle light made a magical color in the fresh, clean air — like the world was new again.

She still had to find out about Rusty.

She wondered, too, if he was thinking of her.

It had looked a little like rain, and it being Saturday anyway, the haying crew quit early, and Rusty and Grady Simmons went home and hurriedly cleaned up, then met downtown. Rusty walked from his house in town, and Grady, who lived a few miles out, hitched a ride. They would go to the weekly picture show behind Reinhardt's Trading Company. Grady had some makings, so they would sit in the front row and smoke. That always impressed the girls.

They sat down on the bench in front of Shorty Yandell's grocery store, now closed for the day. The sun was out strong again, but was low, and the shade from the building lay in the gravel street before them.

Music blared from a few blocks away — a familiar male singing voice flowing out of a large horn atop a car that rolled slowly through town. "Deep with-innnn my heart, lies a melodeee ... ."

"Well, the Showman's here," Grady said. The motion picture would be shown just around the corner, with chairs set up in front of the projector that would beam the images on the back of the plastered rock store building. People would soon be coming in — some in cars, a few with wagons and teams and on horseback and several on foot, carrying lanterns that they would light for the trip home.

Grady stamped out his cigarette butt and spat in the dust. "One of these times, I'd like to go to Okmulgee and see a modern motion picture in a real theater. I always wanted to see 'King Kong.' But guess these old picture shows beat nothin'."

"Yeah. We'll go pretty soon so we can get a seat up front," Rusty said. "Before it gets dark, we can look back and see if there are any girls we don't know."

"You better be careful, hadn't ya? Maggie might find out," Grady said. He grinned, baring yellow teeth.

"Ha! You think I'm worried about that? Ain't no girl got her hooks in me yet."

"Oh, ya mean you're like that *other* Bob Wills song, huh? You know, where he says 'I'm too young to marry . . . .'" Grady drug the words out and grinned again.

"You bet! I got a lot to do before I settle down. I'm free, white and twenty-one – well, almost twenty-one. Besides, it don't hurt to look around."

Thunder in the Heartland

"Heck, if I had a girl as pretty as yours I wouldn't be lookin' at all. Say, I hadn't seen her for a while. Is she off visitin' kinfolks or somethin'?"

He nudged Rusty with his elbow. "And tell me somethin', you and Maggie – are you . . . ? You know . . . ."

Rusty's face felt hot, the way it did when some other guy said anything about Maggie. He stood up and ran his comb through his hair. "Come on. We better go before the front row gets filled up."

He felt the usual excitement as people of all ages lined up to pay the few coins to sit in the open and see whatever was showing – likely some silly, black and white cartoon, a scary serial with somebody like Bella Lugosi, then probably a cowboy movie. The crowd never seemed to mind, if they even knew, that the pictures were old, even some that didn't have words with them.

Normally it was pleasant watching the movie under the stars, with usually enough of a breeze to keep the mosquitoes away. But now it looked like rain again. Dark clouds had built up and marred a pretty sunset.

Rusty and Grady walked over to where the manager – a man wearing city dress pants and a shirt with short sleeves – was standing with one of his two assistants a little out of earshot of the crowd. He was looking to the west and said to the helper, "Hell! It's gonna rain like a cow pissin' on a flat rock."

"It might do a lot worse than that," the other said. "I sure don't like the looks of them clouds. We can try it, I guess."

The movie started with the usual cartoon about little animals singing and playing. Rusty and Maggie had sat here many times and laughed and held hands – his mind all through the movie being on when he would drive her in his dad's Packard out to the City Well. It was a pump and rock affair built by the WPA on a little hill, and was a dandy place to park.

Finally, there had been the night last summer. A

rounded half moon was up, and a breeze made it just cool enough with all four windows rolled down. After that, he carried a blanket in the car — it was less cramped and better outside on the ground.

He thought of those times over and over, but it was the night of the rounded half moon that Rusty knew he would never forget in all its detail.

And now he wished he could. He had experience, of course, and had been the first for her, as he knew he would be, and that thrilled him even more – though it bothered him, too.

Constantly, it seemed, he heard her voice, felt her touch, and saw her clear blue eyes and turned-up nose that gave her a little-girl look, and her scattered freckles that he kidded her about. He did look at other girls, but saw only her — and the thought of her with another guy, he couldn't stand.

He didn't know why he had never told her all that. During most of the time they spent talking, he had wisecracked, or argued with her about little things, like her odd ideas.

If only she hadn't told him she was pregnant. He first had accused her of lying – but had the nagging feeling that she wasn't. It was too big a decision to make, and in too little time. His dad wanted him to go to the agriculture college at Stillwater – though he hated studies and had barely made it out of high school – then go into the feed business with him. And there were so many other things he wanted to do.

Besides, as hard as he tried, he couldn't picture himself bringing her home to meet his parents – even without considering the shotgun-marriage embarrassment. She was too shy around most people, didn't wear good clothes, and her dad was a sharecropper who also hauled junk and did odd jobs.

He and Maggie had talked about it, of course, but the discussions always ended unsettled and with bitter words and hurt feelings – usually hers. And he would say he would think about it later.

Finally, she told him she would leave soon. It was the only thing to do. Besides, her father gave her no choice.

That was when she had clung to him and, for the first time, begged him to take her away. She held onto him until he pushed her away, aware of her wetness left on his shirt. It was their last time together.

The sound stopped, and numbers and crazy markings flicked across the screen. Grady and other guys around them immediately hooted and whistled – it was one of the fun parts of the movie, when a new reel had to be put on. Rusty didn't join in this time.

It started sprinkling and lightning flashed. And the Showman, along with most of the audience, decided it was a good time to give it up. He said something about people holding on to their tickets till next week's picture show as they began leaving.

Soon, Rusty and Grady stood in the shelter of his family's large front porch, listening to the rain.

"Heck, I sure wanted to see the rest of the movie – I like Johnny Mack Brown," Grady said. "Anyhow, I'm glad we didn't get a bad storm."

Rusty was wondering about that – if the storm had hit where Maggie was. And it could have, as her aunt didn't live that far away. Even if he never saw her again, he wanted to know she was safe.

Never see her again? And what if she wasn't safe? What if . . . .

He knew then he could never forget her. Not only was her face branded in his brain, but their many times together, even the last one when she cried – a memory that verily squeezed his heart – all were permanent landmarks in his life; pictures in his mind that would never fade. She had changed his life as nothing had before. She was part of him — he would never feel whole without her.

And regardless of whether she was going to have a baby, he needed her, probably even more than she needed him. He could hardly wait to see her, and tell her he would marry her – to beg her to marry him if he had to.

But if only it wasn't too late!

Maggie learned that Rusty was unhurt from Homer Riddle, a pleasant, rather young-looking man who came by in a Model A.

Just makin' sure everybody's accounted for," he said, smiling as he stepped over the broken picket fence. "We were lucky – no injuries anywhere in town. And they say this is the only place in the state that got any damage. Looks like the twister just dipped down right here, then took off."

Aunt Lottie introduced them. Homer was a rural mail carrier and helped his father farm, as well as being director of the young people's class in her church. Maggie decided he was eight, maybe even ten years older than her.

"Soon as I deliver the mail, I'll come back and help you start cleaning up," he said, speaking to both of them, but looking at Maggie.

He turned before getting in his car and looked at her again. "Anything I can do to help you get settled here, let me know. I know this whole community." He blushed.

Aunt Lottie went about picking up things here and there, talking happily as she did. In a strange moment, Maggie saw her aunt as she never had before. It wasn't so long ago that this was not an old woman, who now had little to worry about except cleaning up after a storm.

Also, Maggie saw herself as she hadn't before. Someday, she, too, would be at a different age, without worries and sorrows that, at the present, were about to devour her.

Life changes — but never really changes.

Maggie was sure Rusty had heard about the storm damage here, and had wondered about her. At one time, that would have excited her.

She was glad, too, that he was all right, although she didn't plan on seeing him again.

But if she did, it would be the last time, and she would

try hard to explain it to him. She had made a decision, and had never felt so right about anything. It was almost the way her aunt thought about Providence.

It wouldn't be easy, especially at first, raising her child alone. And she knew she would miss Rusty at times. But, like the storm, it would pass.

She began helping Aunt Lottie. And she knew her aunt was right. She *would* look back at this time and smile.

The following recognizes Oklahoma's longtime love affair with the horse, along with those ubiquitous figures on the rural scene of yesteryear: the traveling horse traders.

To Ride in a Vapor

Dennis, along with Bo Higby and DeWitt Merrifield, was at the front of the crowd of men as the first horse was unloaded. They had beat it to the vacant lot the minute they saw the two flatbed trucks with the high sideboards roll in, their motors whining as they rumbled over the gravel street. The commotion had enlivened a quiet summer afternoon, and for Dennis and his two pals, meant the biggest day of the year — the horse traders were in town.

"Gents, he's a five-year-old, and as good a saddle horse as you'll find," said the one known as Jack the Jockey as he led a gaunt blue roan in a small circle. "He's worth a hundred, but right now I'll take sixty-five cash money. And I guarantee ya, I won't be makin' six bits. Business is slow. It's the war, I reckon."

To Dennis, the word didn't mean much – he had heard his father and other people talk over and over about a war going on with the Germans and the Japs. It meant even less today.

"What ya lookin' for in a trade, Jack?" said a man in overalls, standing close to Dennis. He smelled of sweat and chewing tobacco.

"Oh, I might take a decent mule or workhorse, with a little boot."

Bo whispered, "That ol' plug looks a lot older than that, don't he?"

"Yeah, and he's probably wind-broke," DeWitt said. "Probably couldn't lope from here to the train depot."

"He's mangy, too. I bet Jack got 'im over around Ticky Ridge."

Both laughed. Dennis looked at them and laughed, too. They were older, and he respected their judgement.

Not far away, Jack the Jockey's two partners were unloading the other truck while a few women unfolded a large tarpaulin and set out apple crates packed with pots and pans and groceries. The traders would be camped there for a few weeks, maybe months, their stock picketed or hobbled close by.

Dennis loved being here. He had started to Willa Dean Ramsey's house when he saw the traders rolling in. He and Willa Dean had been playmates since they were small, and both his and her families teased them about being sweethearts. She'd understand why he hadn't come over.

"Wish Jack would let us ride a few of 'em," DeWitt said. "Fred and Bob used to let me ride their horses. They had some pretty good ones, too. Remember them, don't ya?"

"Yeah, and I remember 'Horse Trader' Phillips, too – F.O. Phillips, his real name was. Used to come in a team and covered wagon, leadin' five or six horses," Bo said.

He grinned and looked at Dennis. "I even got to stay all night in that little wagon once – me and his son, Joe, paled around a little. And I'd get woke up every time one of them horses scratched its rump on the wagon. The whole rig would shake, and the old man would holler, 'Get away from there!'"

All three laughed, especially Dennis. He couldn't imagine being lucky enough to stay all night in a horse trader's wagon, but was glad that he, too, remembered the ones they talked about — Fred Brookshire and Bob Scritchfield, who had trucks, and even Mr. Phillips and his wagon. Dennis could even barely recall a family of traders who came in a little house on wheels — people called it a gypsy wagon. The old woman had a monkey on a chain, and, so he heard, told fortunes.

A loud and familiar voice broke the spell of the moment. "I didn't like the looks of that Phillips kid! I said I'd whup 'im if they ever came back." It was Emory Fain, who lived with an uncle and aunt out in the country and always wore dirty clothes, and somehow hardly ever had to go to school. He was even bigger than Bo and DeWitt, and was ugly anyway, and had a way of grinning that everybody hated – his lips would pull back and curl, showing his upper gums.

Bo and DeWitt didn't answer, pretending to listen to what Jack the Jockey was saying. Finally, Emory muttered something else and lumbered off.

"About ridin' these horses," Bo said. "I don't know if I'd wanna get on any of these ol' plugs anyhow. I bet some of 'em are pretty rank."

"Oh, they're probably half crazy," DeWitt said, "but I don't think it'd take a Todd Whatley to ride any of these sorry ol' horses."

"Guess that's right," Bo said. "If any of Jack's horses had any real buck in 'em, he'd sell 'em to them Beutler brothers out at Elk City."

"Ha! The Beutlers wouldn't want anything Jack's got. They've got a first-class rodeo company."

Dennis looked up at DeWitt. "Where do these horses come from?"

"Oh, I guess Jack gets a few little ol' Choctaw ponies nobody else wants, and no tellin' where he finds these other nags. But most of 'em are about ready for the glue factory."

Dennis wasn't sure what he meant. He turned his attention back to Jack the Jockey.

That's when the little spotted horse was unloaded. It was exactly what Dennis had long dreamed about, even down to every spot — white on its face and just the right places on its sorrel body. It was slick and slender – though not poor; and not stocky like a Shetland – yet not nearly as tall as horses that grown men rode.

Mainly, though, the horse had a special look. There was something about his neck and head – when he turned just so, except for his color, he looked like Red Ryder's horse in the funny papers. And his eyes were open wide and curious, like a kitten's, but friendly, too – and, Dennis was sure, once or twice looked right at him.

Dennis had never seen a horse like this before, and knew he never would again. He even thought of a name: Beauty.

"A pretty good-lookin' little horse, and looks young enough, but a paint ain't much good," DeWitt said.

"What's wrong with 'em?" Bo said.

"Solid-color horses are best, that's all. Look at Gene

A typical horse-trading scene in a small Oklahoma town, circa 1945. Photo courtesy, Joe Phillips.

Autry's horse, Champion. And Tom Mix – what's his horse, Tony? And all the good rodeo ropers and bulldoggers, they ride solid-color horses — Ike Rude, John McEntire and guys like that."

"Well, Cecil Cornish, his horse is spotted – Smokey, a rodeo trick horse," Bo said. "Besides, what about the Cisco Kid? Ain't his horse spotted?"

"Yeah, but you know that tall paint horse ol' Charlie Whitewater rides into town, the one with a glass eye? Nobody can get near 'im, not even the blacksmith. Nobody but Charlie, that is. I don't know how he rides 'im."

"Maybe that's because Indians are that way – I've heard they teach their horses not to let strangers get on 'em."

Dennis no longer cared what his older pals thought. He turned and ran for the post office to talk to his father, praying he wouldn't be too late. He *had* to have Beauty!

The little horse rode even better than he looked. He swept down the road in a soft little trot that was more like a skip, and at the tiniest shake of the reins or the right sound from Dennis, would ease into a lope, then into a smooth gallop. And the instant he knew Dennis wanted him to, he would lay back his little ears, point his nose straight out and beat the earth in a dead run, his long mane flowing.

He not only seemed to recognize his name, whatever he might have been called before, but quickly learned to respond to Dennis' spoken and physical commands, turning almost before Dennis signaled by leaning or by using his knees. It was like Beauty knew what his young master was thinking, and loved doing everything he wanted.

Dennis thought he would burst with pride every time he stood back and looked at his horse tied up in front of one of the stores downtown. He looked flashy with the saddle, but had a specially pretty way of standing — hip-shot like other horses, yet more graceful, his pretty neck arched as he looked about, his curious kitten eyes always alert.

But what Dennis loved most was just being near Beauty, whether feeding, brushing or petting. He often walked out to see him in the pasture, putting his face against his soft nose and talking to him, and then swinging up on him, bareback. And while the animal grazed Dennis would lie on his back facedown, his eyes closed as he savored the knowledge that Beauty was his, enjoying even the rich smell of the wonderful little horse.

He would always take good care of Beauty, as he had promised his father when he agreed to buy him.

One pretty morning when he rode past Levi Grayson's lot at the edge of town, he thought about this. The "dead wagon," as people called it, was there to take away a dead horse. The animal was just over the fence, and Dennis got a good look at it as a man, after chasing away some dogs, hooked a chain or something onto it so it could be hoisted into the truck. The horse was all bloated, its two legs on one side pointing straight out and skyward. Its eyes were wide open and glazed and its teeth showing, like it was grinning in some awful way.

Beauty shied and jumped sideways. Dennis wanted to get away, too, so he lifted his little horse into a lope. "Just an old, old horse, boy," he said, and patted Beauty on the neck.

One fall day, Dennis came home from school and found Beauty sluggish-like. He brushed him good and rode him, but his ears didn't stand up like they had, and his gait lacked its smooth rhythm and occasionally was even rough and choppy.

The next day, the little horse wouldn't eat. And if he recognized Dennis at all, he didn't show it.

Dennis' father had Kermit Jackson, the community's unofficial animal doctor, come and look. Kermit said the horse likely had a little colic, but to let him know if he wasn't better in a few days.

The next day, Dennis went straight downtown from school. He had promised Willa Dean he would buy her a Pepsi in Middleton's Store while she explained a homework assignment to him. He was lucky she liked him. She was a straight-A student.

As they walked down the sidewalk, he saw Emory Fain stomping toward him and grinning. He couldn't imagine what Emory Fain was going to say, but had a bad feeling about it.

Emory stopped right in front of him, grinning even bigger and showing more gums. "That little spotted horse of yours, he's dead. I just went past your pasture and seen 'im. A bunch of dogs are eatin' out his hind end."

Dennis wanted to think it was Emory's idea of a mean joke, but somehow he knew it wasn't. Instantly, he saw Beauty — bloated, eyes open and glazed, teeth showing in an awful way; and he fought to blot out the picture of the dogs.

He flew into Emory, pounding at the disgusting, grinning face with his fists, knowing as he did he wasn't doing any damage.

Dennis was blinded by the sudden pain to his nose as he heard Emory's mocking laughter. He went backwards over a bread box, and as he fell tasted the blood that ran down his face with tears. Willa Dean and several spectators around him were a blur. He lay there, dizzy and sick.

He would have felt humiliated, but he no longer cared.

A few years after his horse died, Dennis, when not in school, spent considerable time with Willa Dean, who now was not only his girl, sort of, but his closest friend. And he read. That included the news, and he still occasionally read the funnies – except for Red Ryder.

Kermit Jackson had said the horse might have been sick before the traders sold it, and speculated about various horse ailments. To Dennis, it didn't matter; Beauty was gone.

Dennis didn't mess around downtown with the other guys anymore, and if the horse traders still came every year, he didn't notice.

When he was home, he stayed to himself, often reading or listening to the radio, either on the shady part of the front porch, or in his upstairs room.

His parents were understanding, but his little sister, Carrie, wasn't. The latest thing she had bothered him with was her project to build a house for her puppy. She nagged him daily.

"Carrie, that pup can sleep in the shed. He doesn't need a house!" he would tell her.

"Yes, he does, too! He needs a little house of his very own," she would say, sounding like she was about to cry.

"Okay, maybe tomorrow." He had said that several times.

One day Dennis, and virtually everyone else at school, heard the big news: President Truman had decided the United States would drop the atomic bomb and end the war. Dennis rushed home to read the afternoon paper and turn on the radio to learn more about it.

And there, his mother told him something else: Emory Fain, who several months before had left for the Army, had been killed in action. His uncle had been notified; he was to pick up the body at the train depot the very next day.

A few days later as Dennis and Willa Dean walked home from school, she said, "I know why you're so quiet. You feel bad about Emory Fain, don't you? Even though you hated him."

"I wish I had taken better care of my horse, for one thing. And I wish people didn't have to go off and get killed in wars," Dennis said.

"It wasn't your fault your horse died – and it's not your fault that Emory's dead. He died in the war, not because you didn't like him. Mrs. Woolridge in my English class says it's natural for people to feel regret, and guilt, especially during times of death."

"It just seems like too much has happened in the last few years," he said. "And it's all hard to understand. How can life be so perfect, and then start changing all of a sudden?"

"Mrs. Woolridge would say that's all part of growing up. She says things change by the day, sometimes for the good and sometimes for the bad – and that we have to make the best of the good while we have it."

Willa Dean's words didn't mean much to Dennis.

He did decide, though, he would go home and help Carrie build her doghouse and get it over with. And he hoped she grew up and learned how to handle sadness before the dog died.

Emory's funeral was held in the school gym. Even though Emory Fain never went to school much, it was decided he was a war hero and the services should be held there.

The coffin was closed. Still, Dennis imagined how Emory must have looked before they did whatever they do to dead people – with eyes open and glazed, and teeth bared so that, even not considering his gums, his face would be in a ghastly grin.

The preacher paraphrased the Bible: "Life is only a vapor . . . ." Dennis wondered if even the preacher knew the truth of that. Whether from age, sickness or war, death came — to everything.

Outside after the service, Bo Higby walked up to him. "Too bad about Emory, ain't it?" he said. "I'm lucky. Another few months and *I'd* had to go."

Dennis remembered that Bo was a few years older than him. They hadn't seen each other in a while, and now it seemed he had caught up with Bo in maturity. "Yeah, and I'm luckier – I didn't even have to worry about it."

"Nobody liked Emory much, but it's too bad anyhow," Bo said.

"Yeah, but maybe most of us didn't try to understand him."

"What? I heard about that fight — how he really cleaned your plow. So why do ya say that?"

"Well, maybe as you grow up you look back and start regretting things — things you should have understood, things you wish you'd done or hadn't done . . . I don't know,

I guess sometimes I just wish I could make time stop and stand still for a little while."

"Come to think of it, sometimes I wish that, too, but it don't do no good to keep wishin' stuff like that. When ya do, you're just beatin' a dead horse." Bo caught himself, and grinned slightly with embarrassment. "I mean . . . I wish I hadn't said it that way."

Dennis wished he hadn't, either. But he knew Bo was right.

"White Ella" is another story that, while fiction, pays homage to the multicultural character of the state, and particularly to a onetime resident of the author's hometown of Oktaha: Ann Freeman – for years better known as "White Annie." This tale was first published in the May/June 1998 issue of **Western Digest** *magazine.*

White Ella

For many years, most people around the little town of Oktoka remembered White Ella as a wrinkled, irascible old woman who lived on the other side of the tracks with the rest of her people, the main thing different about her being her much lighter color.

"Well, here comes ol' White Ella and some more of them niggers," one of the Saturday morning loafers would muse when glancing up from his whittling to see Ella, her grown daughter, Nellie Mae, and a few other colored women walking up the alley between the old livery barn and the Oktoka Mercantile Company. And one of the boys playing near the barn would throw a corncob at them and yell, "Heeeeey, White Ella!" — triggering a string of mutterings and a cussword or two as the youngsters giggled and skedaddled for the hayloft.

But White Ella was more interesting among the whites as a subject of mystery than of mockery. They wondered where she had come from — story upon story had emerged from years of speculation about why the woman, with blue eyes and a nose that freckled when not under a bonnet, had grown up among the Negroes.

One version was that as a child she was captured by the Indians — probably the Kiowas or Comanches — and somehow got mixed up with a few black captives when they were traded back to non-Indians for horses and other valuables.

Another was that she was the illegitimate baby of the daughter of a well-to-do Southern family, and was secretly given to the slaves, who took her with them from Georgia or somewhere when they were brought west to pick cotton in Indian Territory.

But whatever her background, at heart Ella was Negro. She spoke with the same grammar and slow thickness peculiar to her family and neighbors, wore the same tacky, patched-up clothes, walked with the same dragging shuffle and, when downtown, patiently obeyed the custom of being waited on after the white customers in the Mercantile.

White Ella was even a bigger source of diversion around Oktoka than Will Greenley, the town liar. Whiskered and scruffy and always dressed in rags, Will Greenley was nonetheless highly imaginative, and it was said he lied as naturally as he breathed, and probably had never told the truth one time in his whole life.

For example, Will, for many years a widower who lived on the same small, poor farm above Dingy Creek where he grew up, said he was an expert farrier when just a boy, and that one time outlaw Jesse James, returning to Missouri after some holdups in Texas, stopped at his place and had his horse shod — and liked the job so well that he came back over and over when his horse needed shoeing so Will could do it. And every time he paid Will four silver dollars — one for each hoof.

After such a yarn, Will Greenley responded to the hoots of disbelief by staring fiercely at his listeners and, while sputtering snuff, declaring, "That's the truth! I'll swear on a stack of Bibles!"

And when he was out of earshot, the listeners shook their heads and chuckled and said, "Oh, that damn lyin' Will Greenley! He's the windiest man in Oklahoma."

He also had concocted several intriguing theories about White Ella's origin, but there were so many about her that even the colorful Will Greenley couldn't top them all, so his White Ella stories didn't draw much attention.

Until, that is, Will Greenley gave his biggest, and final, account about White Ella — which was his final account about anything. He wrote it in a letter just before he died.

And it was the first believable story Will Greenley ever told — not only because it was considered a deathbed declaration, and because of his uncharacteristic sorrowful comments, but because it contained things that surely no sane person would make up and tell on his own family.

The letter introduced a shockingly different version of the death of prominent pioneer resident Thomas Newsomberry, who settled in the area when Oktoka was established with the laying of the Katy Railway tracks in the early 1870s and acquired Indian land by marrying a Creek woman — and who was killed, according to previous reports, by a drifting cowhand.

But the letter's big astonishment concerned Will Greenley himself: He and White Ella were related.

"I'm telling this because I want to get some things off my chest before I am called Up Yonder, and especially for Ella's sake," his handwritten testimony read. "I didn't tell it before because I promised my mother I wouldn't, but since she's long gone, and I'm old and ailing, and Ella is the only family I got left, I figure I owe it to Ella not to take this secret to the grave. Besides, if I had told it in person around town, nobody would have believed me because of the god-awful liar I've been all my life. And for that I'm sorry."

For weeks, people crowded inside the Mercantile, where the letter, according to directions left by the deceased, was posted, to devour every succulent word and lose themselves in one enthralling mental image after another.

A young rider, who had deserted his boring, sweaty job of herding cattle on the Shawnee Trail, dismounted in front of the commodious two-story house one spring afternoon, aiming to ask for something to eat before moving on and looking for an easier line of work. He was about to knock on the door when he heard the strident voices of a man and woman inside. He eased to the side of the house and crouched under a window and listened.

"But Tom, you said we would get married anyway — you said you were going to leave your wife someday. So now's the time. Don't you ... Don't you love me, Tom?" The woman, who sounded young, was crying as she spoke.

"I told you, Molly, I can't do that, not just now. Of course, I love you — you know I do — but, it's just that ... And you shouldn't be here now at any rate, not this time of day. Molly, right now things are too complicated. You just don't understand. Maybe later. Maybe . . . ." It was a man's voice — more mature, and more refined, than the woman's.

"No, *you* don't understand! I'm going to have your baby, Tom! And 'later' will be too late." She was still weeping, and her voice was now rising in frenzied anxiety. "Tom, please, listen to me. I love you — I *need* you! Please don't leave me!"

The cowboy peeked through the window to see the man, who now had turned away from the girl and was opening the door. The girl's back was to the window. "Molly, go home now. We'll talk later. Hurry — my wife will be coming back from the orchard any minute now. We'll talk later."

As the man, holding the door open, turned to face the young woman again, he caught sight of the cowboy in the window. His eyes widened, then he yanked open a drawer in a nearby table and hauled out a pistol.

But the girl, amazingly quick, grabbed it from his hand — just what was in her mind was hard to say.

"Molly, what the devil are you doing? Give me that gun! Molly . . . ."

The cowboy, a free meal now far from his mind, turned and ran for his horse. The man's voice, as frantic as the girl's had been, grew louder along with the new sounds of a struggle.

Then the cowboy heard a gunshot.

He swung into his saddle and spurred his horse.

As the young man galloped off, the girl, sobbing, her face contorted with panic, stumbled from the house and headed for her family's modest home not few away. If she knew a stranger had been there when she killed her lover, she didn't care.

A posse of citizens had seized a black man who farmed some of Newsomberry's land on shares down in Dingy Creek bottom and were about to lynch him to a cottonwood tree when a U.S. deputy marshal who had followed the fresh horse tracks arrested the cowboy (Will Greenley didn't recall his name). Within a few days the suspect would be taken to Fort Smith and found guilty of murder before Isaac C. Parker, the new U.S. judge for the Western District of Arkansas with jurisdiction over Indian Territory, and hanged.

On the same day the deputy and the young cowboy, hands cuffed in front of him, rode eastward for Fort Smith, Molly was being married in a simple ceremony in her family's yard. She had consented to marry Wilford Greenley, a farmer who also worked on the railroad. He was homely but kind, and a hard worker. And, though he knew she was carrying another man's child, he was giving her the important comfort of marriage.

Several months later, Molly named her baby girl Rosalyn.

About a year later, she had a baby boy. She and her husband called him Will.

But soon Wilford Greenley came to resent the first child. As he doted on his own baby son, he grew more aware that

Rosalyn wasn't really his. He commenced to drink, and became even more resentful.

So Molly, nervous about the situation, began letting Elenora, a neighboring Negro woman and former slave who worked for them occasionally, keep little Rosalyn at her house when Wilford was home. Molly then became sickly, and soon the baby girl was spending more time with Elenora than with Molly and her husband.

Several months later, Wilford Greenley was killed in an accident on the railroad. He had been drinking, and fell in front of a moving engine. There was nothing left, folks said.

Molly continued to let Elenora keep her daughter — now mainly because Molly was weak with her illness, and because of the hardship of caring for young Will and trying to farm the poor, rocky soil by herself.

When Will was barely old enough to help support them by working the farm, shoeing horses and mules and doing other work for neighbors, Molly died. People said it was from pure grief — and it likely was, but people didn't know her grief had little to do with losing her husband.

Elenora continued to keep the girl, whom she now loved as her own and had nicknamed "Ella." Elenora was poor, but a strong, decent woman, and she and her husband were able to give the child a good enough home.

Will grew up and got married. Several years later his wife died, and he continued to live on the farm alone. The two never had children.

A long time later — it was several years after statehood — Will decided to go see Ella and discuss the situation.

The two had been more like distant neighbors than family members when growing up, and Ella's foster mother was now dead and she lived with a Negro man and had children — black children — of her own. So the meeting was awkward.

But Ella, a meek and kind person, agreed to keep the family secret, giving up any claim to her share of the Greenley farm, despite the fact she and her family lived in a sharecropper's shack and were needy.

"I hated it that it happened that way, but I was between a rock and a hard place because of my promise to Mamma — I knew back then she would roll in her grave if folks knew she killed Thomas Newsomberry," Will Greenley said in the last page of the letter. "Besides, me and Ella knew how much talk there would be about white folks living with colored folks. So we shook hands on it and kept quiet all these years."

The letter went on:

"Now, Ella knew she was the daughter of the most famous settler in these parts, even if she wasn't legitimate and couldn't claim his holdings. And she knew she *could* have claimed half *my* farm if she spoke up — and now my farm should be worth right smart, since a big outfit is fixing to drill for oil on the place. But she didn't say a word. And because of that, she's a real lady. I'm mighty proud to call her my sister."

He added, "And I'm proud that I finally told this. Now I can go to my Maker knowing that, for once, I've told the truth."

Emotion flooded the white community. Even the most cynical were touched; tears ran down the hardest of faces.

"Poor ol' Will Greenley — he wasn't so bad after all," said one of the loafers downtown. "Even if he did go around looking like the back end of hard times, and if everything else he ever told was a damn lie."

But the majority of pity gushed for the woman people had long known as White Ella, and for whom it wasn't too late to do something. Overnight, White Ella was a celebrity — something Oktoka needed, and had never had — and somewhat of an ambassador, a symbol of goodwill between Oktoka's two cultures that had long been divided by the railroad tracks.

Community leaders tried to see that she got her share of the Greenley place, but couldn't find out anything about

---

any oil, and learned the property would be sold for past-due taxes.

But they would at least recognize the poor woman. Everyone started being nice to White Ella — if that was what they should call her now. The last name, too, was in question, since she had received her mail under different names, and the whites customarily didn't recognize last names of Negro women, as it was believed most of them weren't legally married. Many people now simply called her Ella, but others said "Rosalyn" or "Miss Greenley" or "Mrs. Greenley" — sometimes even "Miss Newsomberry" or "Mrs. Newsomberry."

When Ella and her party came walking up the alley, the loafers would stand from their benches and say, "Good mornin', ma'am." And boys playing around the old livery barn kept their mouths shut.

At the Mercantile, people held the door for her, and she got waited on right away. Similar courtesies went to Nellie Mae and others with her.

Soon all the people from that side of the tracks were viewed as fellow humans. And when near the whites, those people acted even more polite than usual.

White Ella seemed pleased, but puzzled, by it all.

Especially when members of the Oktoka Ladies Club invited her to one of their meetings. Ella came, in a patched, but clean and starched-stiff dress, but was so ill at ease she hardly said a word except to mumble thanks for the tea and cookies. Then when finished, she busily gathered and carried all the dishes to the kitchen.

"No, no, honey, you don't have to do this — you're our special guest!" the host said.

But Ella kept washing the dishes, now composed and smiling and oblivious to the stir of embarrassment around her.

Ella was also a dignitary on her own side of the tracks, where at church meetings she was asked to lead the singing and at every funeral — typically a celebrated affair when soda pop was sold from ice boxes out front and the singing was especially loud — she was urged to take part.

"Yessuh, poor ol' Sister Washington passed the other day — she was an important deaconess in our church," one of the black women, while ordering several cases of soda pop in the Mercantile, answered when asked if someone had died. "An' Miss Ella, she's gonna come and say some eulogy words."

It became common for one of the loafers downtown to say, "Wonder who died over in nigger town — uhhh, I mean over in the colored section?" referring to all the dressed-up commotion in front of one of the old frame churches over there, and the ensuing vigorous singing on the inside.

"Do what? Oh, I don't know. Just some old darky," another would say. "All I know is, White Ella is preaching the sermon."

Ella died some years later — it was after the Great Depression, when several residents had moved out to California, and people were now talking about World War II — and the funeral of all funerals was held across the tracks. Cars, along with wagons and teams, were parked up and down the dusty street in front of the church, the singing was thunderous, and probably more cases of pop were sold than in all the Negro community's funerals combined. Even a few whites attended, and stood in back of the jam-packed building, fanning themselves on the warm summer day.

But the Ladies Club got Ella's family to agree that Ella would be buried in the whites' cemetery. The Ladies Club, along with the local Masonic Lodge, would provide for the plot and burial. And money was raised for a headstone, with some words about Ella being the descendant of local pioneers.

However, when the stone was ready, the roads were icy, then muddy, so hauling the stone to the cemetery was delayed. And interest in the project ebbed — after all, an old mystery was solved; the book on Ella, so to speak, had been closed with the covering of her grave. So the stone remained where it had been temporarily placed in the back of the Mercantile — and where it would become more or less forgotten among sacks of feed, horse collars and rolls of hog wire.

And it turned out that was just as well.

Some years later — people were listening to Hank Williams sing "Hey, Good Lookin'" on the radio, and there was a war of some kind in Korea — an elderly but well-dressed and well-spoken woman, and who showed her Indian heritage, paid a visit to Oktoka.

She told people in the Mercantile that she lived in Houston and this was her first time back to Oktoka since she grew up in the area, and was compiling her family's history — a "genealogy" project, she said. She identified herself as Rosalyn Vanderbilt — her maiden name was Newsomberry; she was the only child of Thomas Newsomberry.

Right away someone mentioned the story about Ella — though, fortunately, nobody said anything about the stone in the back of the store.

Mrs. Vanderbilt laughed, and told a story of her own – which threw the whole matter into confusion, and refuted virtually all of Will Greenley's account.

Some of his report was true, she said — Wilford Greenley *did* drink, for instance. But he wasn't killed by a train engine. He was fired for being drunk on the job, and wound up picking apples in Washington state, where he died many years later.

"That *damn* lyin' Will Greenley!" most people said. That was his way, all right — mixing just enough actual names and facts into his long-winded fibs to leave his listeners mixed up and thinking he just *might* be telling the truth.

A few residents, though, had trouble discounting the story they had accepted almost like Scripture. What earthly reason, they asked, would someone have for telling such a fabrication?

"Hell fire!" the others countered. "When did Will Greenley *ever* need a reason to tell a lie?"

A decade or so later — people were still talking about

---

the assassination of President Kennedy, and the old Mercantile had dwindled to a small store selling only a few groceries, cigarettes and canned soft drinks and beer — a teenage girl named Drucella Tolbertson became the first black student to attend Oktoka High School. It was during the time people were talking about "desegregation," and the school on the black side of the tracks was about to close — but she was chosen as the first to come over to the previously all-white school because of her high scholastic achievement.

A few years later, young Drucella graduated with honors, coming in close behind the valedictorian and the salutatorian.

That's when it came to light who she was. The girl's family, including her grandmother, Nellie Mae, couldn't have been prouder.

There was a ripple of excitement among the few white residents who were old enough and capable enough to remember Ella.

They even talked of erecting the headstone. But as the Mercantile had gradually fallen and been torn down, they reasoned it would never be located in the pile of other stones.

But the important thing, they agreed, was the fact that Will Greenley - regardless of how much of his story was true, and even if he didn't realize it himself — *had* told the truth about one thing: Ella was a lady.

To most residents, though, Ella was still more memorable as a mystery.

One Saturday morning a few older white men were talking in front of the small Cash n' Dash store, near where the old Mercantile had been, while on the inside a clerk watched television behind the counter and youngsters played a noisy electronic game.

One man glanced over to a vacant lot where once had been a frame building. "I'll never forget that old livery barn," he said. "Remember the corncob fights and all the fun us boys used to have over there?"

Another said, "You know, that makes me think of White Ella. Wonder where on earth she came from?"

In the summer of 1950, a dapper, smooth-talking city slicker, introducing himself as F. Bam Morrison, came to the small town of Wetumka and hornswoggled the local folks. But they soon laughed it off, and for more than half a century have had fun commemorating their embarrassment with an annual "Sucker Day" celebration. By fictionalizing the con man and his capers, the author had fun, too.

H. Slam Garrison

I'll tell ya, there's a fella named H. Slam Garrison who better not ever get off the bus in this town again. Not that he's likely to, of course. I think about H. Slam every time a stranger like you stops by — not that you're anything like him, of course; it's just that not many people stop here anymore. It's hard to believe how that man got so well-known in the five or six months he was here. And then the terrible thing he did just before he left.

The first time I saw H. Slam Garrison was when he arrived here one pretty spring day — the bus station was downtown then; I think it was the Union — and I guess everybody on Main Street knew right off he was a salesman. He was middle-aged, and chubby, and could have been from anywhere — you couldn't tell by his talk, which sounded real proper and nice. He was a snappy dresser, and you got the idea he never needed a shave or a bath, and no matter how hot or windy or nasty the weather, never had one of his gray hairs out of place and always looked and smelled, as they say, like he just stepped out of a band box.

And he had a friendly, smooth way about him that made you forget right off that he was a stranger.

That's what made 'im such a good salesman — and he was a crackerjack, I'll tell ya. He sold advertising, mainly, so called on the businessmen every day. He stayed close by, in that old hotel over there — of course, the building's condemned now, but it used to be real nice. Besides the standard stuff like Coca-Cola signs, pictures of pretty girls in new swimsuits, and posters of movie stars smokin' Chesterfield cigarettes, H. Slam always had "special" things to sell — ads in magazines and pamphlets, calendars, little rotating clocks with the merchants' names on 'em, business cards, little games to put on store counters, and more stuff than you could shake a stick at.

He was full of ideas, too. He was real good at dreamin' up "benefits," as he called 'em — you know, something for the good of the town, or to help somebody. Of course, he always took a little off the top for himself. Oh, he was a slick one, I'll tell ya!

I don't know that he ever cheated anybody outright, but he was a real promoter — one of them fellas who'll do anything to get by without workin' at a steady job, you might say. Most storekeepers got where they hated to see H. Slam comin', then usually bought something just to get rid of 'im.

But you couldn't help but like ol' H. Slam, and he pulled a few stunts people around here still laugh about.

Like one time he sold hundreds of calendars to old Uncle Joe Brady at the hardware store — way more than the store could possibly get rid of before the year was out. These calendars had a funny picture for every month — you know, one showed a bunch of no-account, lazy-lookin' characters loafin' around in a machine shop, and under it was printed somethin' like "Our Engineering Department is working hard for you!" Well, H. Slam talked Uncle Joe into buyin' so many, the store wound up sendin' calendars to every person in the county — you couldn't go anywhere without seein' one or two — and the pile of calendars still looked as big as it did to start with, so a bunch of 'em was just dumped behind the store.

Poor old Uncle Joe was mad as a wet hen, but everybody else got a big kick out of it — since the way it happened was a whole lot funnier than the pictures on the calendars. That was the talk in Bud Smith's barbershop for years.

But I'll tell ya, H. Slam could sure do things in a flashy way.

Like when he started a big patriotic project — "to recognize the war heroes of the community," the way he put it. He mentioned he was a veteran himself, though not any kind of a hero — and it was plain, of course, that to him it was just another promotion.

He got all the merchants to donate, and got school kids to peddle little red, white and blue ribbons all over town — and even had the kids go down to Jennings Appliances of an evenin' once a week and hit up the fellas standin' out front — you know, TV was new then, and they'd crowd around to watch baseball and wrestlin' through the store window. And, of course, with somebody there collectin' money, they'd think the store was behind the fund drive, and feel obligated to throw somethin' in the bucket. Oh, that H. Slam was slick, I'll tell ya!

Well, in a few months, that statue of a soldier was put up in the town park, with names of boys from around here who lost their lives in the military engraved underneath, and plans were made to dedicate it on the next Fourth of July. It musta cost a few thousand, at least. You musta seen it when you drove in, down past the old movie theater.   It really stands out in a little ol' dried-up town like this — even with the weeds grown up around it — and when strangers like you come through, they notice it, and sometimes even stop and take pictures.

To us who live here, though, it's just a reminder of that ol' con man, H. Slam Garrison.

But the biggest thing H. Slam did was to get the Youth

Center built. I guess the kids told 'im they didn't have anything to do when school was out for the summer, so he started a big fund drive.

Well, he got the local processing plant to donate a whole lot of peanuts, then sent the kids out sellin' little bags of nuts, with "Goobers for Good Kids" printed on each sack. And he promoted a pie supper at the schoolhouse, and got a farmer to donate a Poland China shoat to be raffled off after all the pies were auctioned. The pig was in a crate and had a pretty ribbon around its neck and a sign under it that said "Rootin' for Youth."

He hit up the merchants, too, of course, and even got Olen Scoggins at the newspaper to print all the contributors' names every week — which, of course, put the pressure on them who hadn't kicked in, so pretty soon just about everybody had.

Well, when the Youth Center was finished, H. Slam started givin' classes there on things like "citizenship, public speakin', art, and literature appreciation" — seemed like that man could do anything. He did it for free, probably with the kids agreein' to help him with his next promotion. It was late summer and the advertising business was slow anyhow.

That's when the trouble started involvin' Buster Worley and his stepdaughter, which led to the worst tragedy in the history of this community.

Buster Worley worked at the peanut processing plant and did odd jobs, and lived in an old two-story house at the edge of town with the stepdaughter, Patricia Worley, who was about seventeen. She went by his last name, maybe because her mother wasn't married before, I don't know.

Buster's wife, the girl's mother, had died about a year before in what musta been a freak accident at home. She musta had something wrong with her for a long time, and had dizzy spells, because I understand she was always fallin' and gettin' bruised up. Finally, the way I heard it, she walked in her sleep one night and fell down the stairs and broke her neck.

Now, Buster, as everybody knew, took a drink now and then, and had a temper — but I always knew 'im as a hard worker, and a good ol' boy, and his wife's death musta been hard on 'im.

Well, it was plain to the teachers and others who knew the girl, she wasn't happy, either. She musta grieved about her mother, probably even more than Buster did, and maybe it was hard on her havin' to do all the housework and cookin'. And I can imagine how Buster might've got on her nerves, comin' in every day all sweaty and smellin' like chewin' tobacco and whiskey.

But I guess Buster tried to be a good father, and he was real protective of that girl, especially since she was growin' up. I wouldn't call her pretty — she had a sad, tired look about her — but she might've looked all right if she'd had better clothes, and she *was* developin' nice, you might say.

In fact, the girl might've had dizzy spells like her mother

Gail Pack, a Sucker Day Queen. Copyright 1977, The Oklahoma Publishing Company.

had, since she came to school sometimes with bruises — and a few of the old busybodies in town started some talk that Buster had been "makin' advances" on her, as they put it. Wasn't that an awful thing to say?

Well, I guess Buster was already in a bad state of mind, with his wife's recent death, and havin' to work hard, and then bein' hit with those ugly rumors — so he musta lost his temper one day when a pair of social workers came to see 'im. I understand he stood on the porch with his twelve-gauge shotgun and told that man and woman to git!

Not that Buster would really shoot anybody — he liked to shoot at a stray cat now and then, and had told it around that he kept his shotgun loaded because he never locked his doors. He wouldn't need a gun against somebody comin' up in broad daylight anyhow, since he was big and tough. They say that when he got mad he'd go to fist city with any-body.

Even though, like I say, he was just a hard-workin', good ol' boy, and I don't think anybody important really believed what those old biddies said about him and the girl.

Anyhow, that little commotion with the social workers caused the sheriff to come up from Holdenville, and some-how it was decided Patricia would stay with one of her teach-ers, until some kind of a court hearing about a month away.

Buster didn't like that, of course, but didn't say much about it for the time bein'.

Well, in the meantime, the girl went to the Youth Cen-ter just about every day, since she musta been impressed by things H. Slam would tell her and the others — H. Slam *did* have a way of sayin' things to impress people.

Another kid who liked the center a lot was George Singingbird. His folks lived down in the creek bottom and were poor as church mice, and he was sort of shy and, I guess, wasn't very good in school — but he took to the art classes like a duck takes to water. Maybe it was because he was half Indian, since I hear some of 'em are good artists. Anyhow, paintin' pictures seemed to come natural to 'im — in fact, I think a few of his pictures are in some museums today.

Anyhow, it seemed like both of those kids found a home, you might say, at the center.

At the same time, H. Slam, who I think had always been a bachelor and never had kids of his own, musta took a likin' to 'em both, and felt like they needed all the help he could give 'em. In fact, you might say those two youngsters became his biggest project yet — and the only one he had around here that didn't involve makin' money. I hear he tried to help 'em with what he called the best "guidance" he could, and told 'em things like "you've got to follow your heart in life, then do whatever you have to do to find happiness." Oh, he was a pretty talker, I'll tell ya!

Meanwhile, the Worley girl and the Singingbird boy — I guess because they felt like they had a lot in common — got sweet on one another, and pretty soon were thicker than molasses.

Now, Buster, like I say, was real protective of the girl, and naturally had always been concerned about what kind of friends she had — and even though for the time bein' she was livin' outside his home, he didn't cotton one bit to her havin' anything to do with George Singingbird.

In fact — of course, I think he had a drink or two and probably didn't mean it — he told it around town one day that he was "lookin' for a certain little 'bird'," and that he was "gonna wring his scrawny little neck!"

Well, that musta scared Patricia pretty bad. I guess she especially worried because, when the boy walked home, as he always did, he had to take the road leading to his family's house in the creek bottom, which went right by Buster's house at the edge of town. She musta talked to H. Slam about it, and I guess he got just as worried, but didn't know what to do other than advise both her and the boy to be extra careful and never be alone anywhere, especially after dark.

And they both *were* careful — except for this one time.

The way I heard the story, Patricia wasn't at the center because the teacher she stayed with wanted her to go to a picture show with her and her husband, and George Singingbird worked late at the center — he was tryin' to finish a painting in time to send it off to some art contest the next day.

Well, the boy started home afoot, like always — except that this time it would be well after dark when he passed Buster's house.

There were no lights on in Buster's house, but his pickup was parked in the yard and his front door was open, so he musta been home — everybody knew he liked to sit down and have a drink and look out for a while after he got home from work. Sometimes that's when he'd see a stray cat.

Then, the way I heard it, H. Slam finally got so worried he took off in a trot, huffin' and puffin', to Buster's house. I guess he'd do anything to protect both those kids, but at the moment probably didn't know how he was gonna help the boy, unless he could talk Buster out of doin' something awful.

Well, the way it was told later, nobody seemed to know for sure who got to Buster's house first, and exactly what happened when they got there.

Anyhow, they say the next morning, Patricia showed up early at the Youth Center, lookin' for H. Slam, and seemed all upset and nervous, like she had something real important to tell 'im.

But H. Slam wasn't there. Then the Singingbird boy came by after mailin' his contest art at the post office, and said he hadn't seen H. Slam that morning, either. Then somebody said H. Slam hadn't been seen at the hotel since the day before.

Well, then it came out that just about dark the evening before, some old folks a few blocks away had heard a shotgun blast — but didn't report it then because they figured Buster was just shootin' at cats.

The way I heard it, Patricia seemed even more upset and nervous, and acted real puzzled by H. Slam bein' gone — but somehow didn't appear exactly worried about 'im.

So she went back to the teacher's house, and the Singingbird boy went home.

Now, get this — a few days later Buster was found inside his house, dead!

Some of the fellas who worked with 'im at the processing plant got to wonderin' why he wasn't on the job. The weather bein' warm, and Buster's old house not havin' any coolin' to speak of, I hear that when they stepped on the porch they knew right off why he hadn't been to work. Poor Buster had been shot with his own twelve-gauge, right in the stomach — they said it really messed 'im up.

Well, they arrested the girl right off. The deputies who came from Holdenville said they could tell she did it because of the calm way she acted — like she was expectin' 'em — and that she didn't seem a bit sorry for what she'd done. Besides, the teacher and her husband said Patricia had changed her mind and didn't go to the picture show with 'em, sayin' she wanted to go to bed early. So the case was, as they say, open and shut.

The deputies figured, to protect the boy, she had slipped into the house before Buster got home from work and waited on 'im, then pulled the trigger as soon as he got inside.

J. Harvey Sipes, her appointed lawyer, said he might enter a plea of self-defense, based on those stories about how Buster treated her, or maybe a plea of insanity — but he said she still likely would get some prison time, the evidence bein' what it was.

But then they turned her loose! Somebody else's fingerprints were all over the shotgun, includin' the trigger! The deputies hadn't checked for prints since they figured it was plain who did it — until the sheriff's office got a letter in the mail, tellin' who did it, and suggestin' the fingerprint check.

The sheriff checked with the War Department, I guess it was, and the prints on the gun belonged to just who the letter said they belonged to — believe it or not, H. Slam Garrison!

And, you know what? Whoever wrote the note did it on a page out of the calendars that H. Slam sold to Brady's Hardware — so there was no way to determine who sent the letter, since everybody and his dog had one of those calendars.

And most of us got a kick out of this part, no matter how tragic the murder was: Whoever sent the letter musta wanted somebody to laugh, because of all the pictures on the calendar, they wrote on the November page, where it showed some ol' hillbilly character holdin' a shotgun, and the words "We aim to please!"

They couldn't find hide nor hair of H. Slam Garrison. They figured he took off right after he killed Buster that night and crossed Junior Tipton's pasture and got to the highway and thumbed a ride — where to, nobody will ever know.

Then, soon after that, it got out that the girl killed Buster after all! At least, she said she did. I understand she confided in her teacher friend, and ... Well, news spreads quick in a town like this.

But the sheriff down at Holdenville didn't believe it, and decided the girl was off her rocker. He said fingerprints don't lie, and kept on huntin' the man who left the prints.

One thing I never understood, though, is how a man could wipe a gun clean — takin' off all of Buster's old prints — then forget to wipe his own prints off after he shot Buster. I guess that was one time H. Slam Garrison wasn't very slick.

Well, the Worley girl and the Singingbird kid finally got married, and had a baby boy. And you know what? She named it after H. Slam, because she said he was one of the few people, besides her mother, who treated her decent — and that he gave her guidance, so she was able to do what she had to do in order to find happiness, or some words to that effect. It's hard to imagine some poor kid with a name like H. Slam, ain't it?

You musta seen the Youth Center when you drove in — except now it's the Senior Citizens Center. There's not many youngsters around here anymore since the school closed some years back — consolidation, they call it.

And nowadays the bus stops over on the highway, and then only if somebody's gonna get on, or off, which ain't often.

When it does stop, though, a few of us around here wonder if we'll see somebody who looks like H. Slam Garrison. But we know we won't. There'll never be another one like him, I'll tell ya.

The following description of a man's obsession with the past also centers on the onetime heart of the typical Oklahoma small town: the general store. The story was first published in the summer of 2001, in ByLine magazine, after it won a first-place award during the annual conference of the Oklahoma Writers' Federation. "Doaksville" here is fictional, and its likeness to any real town is coincidental.

Time Travel, Incorporated

There I sat in this weird-looking apparatus, about to take my first trip in a time machine. I was so excited I hoped my heart didn't stop.

"Remember now, just concentrate on the screen and think of one of your favorite memories," the man said. "And there's absolutely nothing to worry about. Should you become nervous, upset about something you encounter, or for any reason wish to return to the present, simply squeeze the rubber bulb and we'll bring you right back."

He had approached me in the lobby of the retirement center that morning and complimented me on my taste in reading material. I had the latest issue of *Good old Days*.

"You know, a person really *can* go back in time," he said, sitting down beside me and leaning close as if aware of my hearing problem. He introduced himself – his name was

Oscar J. Vanpelt – and said he represented "a new and unique concern" called Time Travel, Incorporated. "But please," he said, lowering his voice and glancing around, "don't repeat that name. Not yet; the company's official announcement hasn't been released." He handed me his card. Only his name and an e-mail address appeared on the card in silvery embossed letters.

I had seen him in the center before and figured he was either a doctor or minister there to visit someone. He was maybe ten years younger than I was, stout but not overweight, and clean-shaven except for a thin mustache. His gray hair had been styled like a movie star's, and not in some everyday barbershop. He was a real dandy in his tan sports jacket, blue necktie, nice casual pants, and shiny shoes.

"You see, many people wish they could return to their golden childhood days. You have, haven't you?"

I smiled and nodded. My wife, God rest her soul, considered that my only fault – I lived in the past, she used to say.

"Consider this," he said, his hands apart as if holding something, like maybe a global representation of the earth. His nails were freshly manicured and he wore a large, glittery ring. "Time is virtually the only phenomenon that remains unexplored – our last frontier, really. For centuries, it's fascinated and challenged our greatest minds, Einstein notwithstanding. Does time move? Or do we move through it? Or is the answer far outside our realm of understanding? In this age of space travel and computers that can do virtually anything, there remains one mystery: time.

"Until now! Now we have Time Travel, Incorporated." He grinned, flashing pearly teeth and an impressive gold inlay. "Ironic, isn't it? The world's most modern advancement deals with the past."

He turned serious again. "Tell me if I'm right. When you close your eyes and see the homey old place where you grew up, for that brief, blissful moment you're truly close to Heaven. Norman Rockwell experienced that – it's obvious in his heartfelt paintings." His eyes narrowed and his voice flowed with understanding. "And you wish you could regress further – to return and actually *feel* the past, to *be* there. Being able to glimpse that beautiful picture of long ago, but knowing you can't step into it and are left hovering on the brink of total ecstasy, is the most frustrating and saddest feeling there is. Am I right?"

My face tingled. He was describing me to a tee! I spent hours alone in my tiny apartment, staring out the window and recalling the happy days in my little hometown of Doaksville. I sifted through old black-and-white pictures and the keepsakes I picked up when the main store was torn down: a tin Prince Albert tobacco can, old newspaper advertisements, even yellowed ledgers and loan contracts bearing the elaborate signature of the merchant, H.W. Rhineberger. He was the town banker, too, the "rich man" of the community.

I was so obsessed with the past that I didn't give a hoot about daily activities at the center. One lady resident talked me into taking some art lessons, but I snorted when she asked me to join the drama club. Playacting for people our age is downright ridiculous.

"I know just what you mean!" I said to Vanpelt, feeling myself grin, silly-like, and blush. "When I was a boy I loved to read *Alley Oop* in the funny papers, about how he'd get in this time machine and . . . "

"Precisely!" he said. "And now that's a reality! Time Travel, Incorporated, has a time machine!"

I guess that's when he knew he had me hooked.

"I can't tell you exactly how it works – the details are handled by our technicians, physicists and mathematicians, as well as our psychiatric and medical staff. But generally speaking, it's like watching a video on the TV screen."

The time traveler, he explained, sits in something resembling a back-massage chair, in an enclosure similar to a hyperbaric chamber used in hospitals, with a pulse oximeter and other devices connected to him. It involves soft music, hypnosis, and the person's own imagination, while his eyes are fixed on the screen. The traveler goes into the past for about six hours at a time, for thirty days.

"You'll go into a trance, you might say, and, for the first time in all your reminiscences, cross a distant threshold – you'll *transcend,* as it were, deeper than you've ever been into the past. Your spirit will *be* there. Of course, you can't interact with people there as the person you are *now*. In other words, you can't change the past. Someday, though, even that might be accomplished."

He promised it was safe. The traveler was constantly monitored and talked in and out of the past by a professional hypnotist. "Nothing can go wrong as long as our system is up – our computers and everything – and it always is. And anytime you wish, you can squeeze a rubber bulb and a buzzer sounds, and the hypnotist will bring you back."

"I guess you've gone back, right?" I said.

"Oh, no, not me. I'm not the nostalgic type. But I cer-

The remains of an Oklahoma small-town general store and adjacent buildings.

tainly empathize with people who are. Besides, I'm always occupied with business. In fact, not many have gone back so far. We have a long list of applicants, but not everyone qualifies. It requires a special person, like you."

"Uh, I guess it costs a lot, doesn't it?"

"Actually, right now the corporation is offering a unique opportunity – a special rate, for a volunteer. You see, the project is still experimental, like the space program. With every endeavor, more is learned, and the project takes a giant step forward. Well, in this case, *backward*." He laughed.

"So I'd be like a monkey on a space flight?"

"No, no! Forgive me if I suggested that analogy. You would simply report your experiences to be recorded in our constant daily research. Of course, you wouldn't have to discuss *personal* details in your past – I mean, for instance, you might relive some romantic episode." He grinned and winked.

"And – the special rate?"

"Now, consider this. It's comparable to getting a seat on the first passenger flight to Venus. Something that only a millionaire could afford. But you could take the thirty-day round of excursions back in time – just think, a virgin odyssey into the past! – for a very modest fee."

"Uh, how modest?"

"I'll have to clear it with the board of directors, but I believe I can swing it for you for as little as, say, ten thousand."

"*Ten thousand dollars?*" I yelped.

"Don't you have that in an IRA?"

"Well, maybe, but . . . "

"All you have to do is sign this agreement. It's the standard liability thing, plus it says you'll take part in the study. And, of course, after thirty days make the token payment of ten thousand to me personally – it's less red tape that way." He whipped a folded paper out of his inside coat pocket, uncapped a Montblanc pen, and flashed his white teeth and gold inlay.

So that afternoon I found myself hooked up to the time machine in the small laboratory of Time Travel, Incorporated. As soon as Oscar J. Vanpelt said "bon voyage" and stepped into his adjoining office, soothing music, along with the every-so-gentle words of the hypnotist, began seeping from the walls.

And it worked, just like the man said!

It was summertime in downtown Doaksville, and little Henry Wilkerson and I were skipping down the street to Rhineberger"s Mercantile. The gravel felt good to the bottoms of my bare feet. We each had a nickel for a big Pepsi or RC. Besides drinking it, we'd put our thumbs in the top and shake it and squirt it at flies on the sidewalk.

In front of the stores, all the fascinating smells were there – a man's pipe, another's fresh chewing tobacco, some sweaty overalls, and the rich fullness of horses and their droppings; a team and wagon were tied nearby. The old loafers appeared, as I remembered, like they would never change. So did the brick and stone businesses, and the homes a few blocks away – simple, but neat, amid flowers and shrubbery. Someday, I lamented, all this would be crumbled store buildings and weedy vacant lots.

Life crept, like the sun. The afternoon dozed. Occasionally would come the clop, rumble and clink of a team and wagon, the ring of a blacksmith's hammer; or a dog lying in the street would lift his sleepy head at the slow approach of a Model A Ford, until it went around him. Otherwise, time stood still.

Later, one of Mr. Rhineberger's sharecroppers plodded in to get groceries, and one of the church ladies tacked up a poster announcing a "rummage sale." I smiled. She didn't know that someday it wouldn't be called that – everyone would have a garage. And finally the shadows lengthened, and eased the day toward evening.

It was Friday, when the picture show came to town. So I hurried home to help my dad do the milking, draw water and slop the hogs, then sat on the back step and scrubbed my feet in a pan. I put on my shoes, washed my face and neck and put on my good shirt.

The movie was outdoors, the image cast on the back of a building by the "show man," a traveling projectionist. For a dime, Henry and I sat on chairs in the vacant lot, waiting to watch stars like Hoot Gibson and Bela Lugosi. When the show started, the mosquitoes came, humming at a high pitch. We swatted at them on hour necks and faces all through the film. It was a long movie.

At home, Mom had me get the kerosene can off the back porch and she doctored my bites. Even with all the windows open, the night was warm and still. I took a quilt out on the front porch and fought mosquitoes again. A breeze came up just before daylight.

Later that morning Henry and I dug some worms and took our poles and walked over to the creek. We caught a few perch. That night I pulled stickers out of my feet and scratched chigger bites. The kerosene helped a little.

The hypnotist's voice brought me out of the past. I had completed my first trip, and as I would each time, I reported my experiences to Vanpelt in his office. With thoughtful nods, he jotted them down.

During my next session, it was fall. There was the distant hum of the cotton gin; wagons and trucks hauled their loads through town. Most of us boys had been raiding watermelon patches, and on cool nights hunting possums – and thinking about Halloween, when we'd go all over town turning over privies.

I was tired of cutting grass all summer – I had forgotten about the hard, sweaty work with those clackity old push mowers. I still had my barnyard chores, and now I had to do them before and after school. On basketball game nights or other special times, I had to carry extra water inside to heat for bathing in a wash tub.

I hated homework, and I had to do it by the light of a kerosene lamp. Doaksville didn't have electricity yet, or indoor plumbing.

I got out of school for a while, though, when I was sick. My folks said it sounded like the whooping cough. Mom applied a sheep-manure poultice, and Dad gave me a spoonful of sugar soaked with kerosene. Both treatments made me try hard not to cough.

After I recovered, I got a toothache. My granddad made me put a wad of his Cotton Boll Twist in my jaw, and I threw up – I knew I would, because I had tried chewing tobacco before, unbeknownst to my folks. By then we had a pretty decent old car, so Mom drove me to a big-city dentist. He drilled and drilled, and finally pulled. If Novocain was invented then, I guess he didn't know about it.

On a later trip, I started liking school when I experienced my first crush on a new teacher, Miss McCutchen. I learned her first name was Leona, and I called her that in imaginary conversations. She looked like a movie star, with clear, blue eyes, a musical voice and a smile that made my tingle down to my toes. I was sure she liked me, too. To impress her, I learned to diagram sentences.

The big pie supper to raise money for the community Christmas tree was coming up, so I worked hard at odd jobs to have enough to buy her pie. I dreamed about sitting close to her and smelling her perfume while we ate.

But when the big event came, I was outbid by some citified jerk who seemed to know her quite well. While everyone in the gym was eating and visiting, she called me over and introduced me to him – they were engaged. "And this," she told him, "is one of my nicest little students." My face was on fire.

I was too old to cry but choked back tears as I walked home, taking a shortcut so I wouldn't meet anyone.

During my next visit back, I was working in the hay harvest one day when I got into it with Mitch Caldwell, the toughest boy in the county. He wanted to fight and I didn't. None of the others called me chicken, but for the rest of the day I felt their looks. A licking would have hurt less.

Several days later, though, out behind the boys' toilet at school, Tommy Ray Fain, a dirty-looking kid who wasn't real bright, called me a bad name, and I gave him a bloody nose. But it didn't make me feel any better, and I decided to tell Tommy Ray I was sorry, someday.

I would always wish I had. One evening when he was on his newspaper route he was hit by a car over on the highway and killed.

The next time I was lulled into yesteryear by the hypnotic voice – which by now I had decided was a recording – I was barely old enough to join the military and there was talk of war. I was also a smart aleck and wanted to get away from my little hick town, so I nagged my folks until they let me sign up early, without finishing high school. For seventeen years my mom, who had little education herself, had dreamed of seeing me graduate. Dad was pretty calm abut it, but as I boarded the train, Mom stood there crying. At the train's first jerk, I almost changed my mind and jumped off.

Fortunately, I would get through the whole war and return home safely. But I'd always see my mother weeping at the depot as the train took her child and her hopes far away. As I relived the moment, the pain was exceedingly sharp. I wished I could, indeed, change history.

I squeezed the bulb, buzzing myself back to the present via the hypnotic voice. Thank Heaven the computer system was up.

That evening I sat in my apartment, feeling low. I wasn't happy after my five trips back to the past, or with this Vanpelt guy, either. It finally had dawned on me that he was the con man of the century, and I was the first monkey in his time-travel project.

He *had* sent me back, though. And he was right about one thing: I had seen my past as I never saw it before. It wasn't that I had any tragedies in my life, but the time behind me wasn't the beautiful picture I once remembered.

And no telling what I'd find in twenty-five more trips.

I had to get out of this mess. Especially since it included a ten-thousand-dollar contract with my name on it.

I sat there brooding while looking through the old souvenirs from my hometown, hating myself because of my mania about the past. Then I had an idea. Maybe I could beat Vanpelt at his own game. He had an obsession of his own: money.

I went to the library and looked up old newspapers on microfilm and made printouts, then stopped at an office supply. When I got back I started applying what little drawing skills I had, and working on my skit.

The next day, after stopping at Kinko's and making a copy of what I'd done, I went to my session on the machine. During my interview with Vanpelt, I mentioned Mr. Rhineberger, and talked at some length about the man's large store, all the farmland he had bought up during the Great Depression, his bank, and his greed for wealth. Some of that was true, but I was creative, too.

The next day I brought copies of the newspaper pages I'd prepared, which contained large ads about Mr. Rhineberger's store and bank. I told Vanpelt they were from my scrapbook, and I thought he might find them interesting.

After the session, I beamed at Vanpelt with all the excitement I could fake.

"Guess what! I actually communicated with someone – you know, *interacted.*"

He looked surprised, but smiled patronizingly. "That's interesting. We'll certainly take note of that."

"It was the banker, Mister Rhineberger," I said. "And not only did we talk, he wants to invest in your corporation! Said he'd like to talk to you about expanding it into selling trips to the future. I told him about the wondrous things we have now. He laughed at first, me being just one of the local overgrown kids, but finally he started listening."

I hesitated for a second and timed my biggest line. "And

he'll pay, he said. One million dollars – in cash! I had no idea that old devil had hoarded up so much."

Vanpelt's expression was changing. For the first time since I'd met him, he didn't appear sure of himself.

"In fact," I said, reaching into my coat pocket, "I was sure you wouldn't mind if I took it upon myself to clinch the deal. I figured maybe you'd give me a commission. So I had him write up and sign a contract. He said he'd only give the money directly to you, though, the boss of Time Travel, Incorporated. He wants you to sign and date your part of the contract and bring it with you. Right away, he said."

I could see the indecision on his face, like he thought maybe the sessions had gotten to me. But he also had the look of greed, or maybe fear of losing a fortune. Finally the greed overcame his fear of his own machine, and he let me hook him up.

I turned on the music, as well as the "hypnotic" voice that I knew by now was his, and I waited about an hour. Then I stepped over and unscrewed the clamps holding the plug in the wall. Smiling to myself about the modern marvel of electricity, I pulled the plug.

When I left, Oscar J. Vanpelt was staring into the blank screen and mumbling.

There was no telling exactly where in the past he'd wind up in his search for Doaksville and Mr. Rhineberger, but I doubted he'd ever get back to the present.

And if he did, I figured he couldn't convince anyone he hadn't forged my signature on some agreement about time travel – any more than he could prove he'd made a one-million-dollar contract with a banker in Doaksville back in 1945.

Wherever he was now, chances are he wouldn't find many painless dentists, and he'd have to get used to haircuts in old-fashioned, Norman Rockwell-type barbershops.

As for me, I still might read about the old days, but I'd definitely live in the present, and that included taking more interest in activities at the center. Playacting, especially.

The following piece of fiction recognizes the fine institution of small-town journalism — but also those public officials in the state who have been corrupt and rascally.

Sam's Big Story

If there was one thing Sam Dodson treasured in life, it was being known as the toughest man in the county — it went along with his reputation as the biggest, the strongest and the bravest. And in all his seventy-something years, more than half of which he had been a lawman, he had never feared anyone, or anything.

Until, that is, he was told he was about to die — not that it was dying he was so afraid of; it was how he was going to be remembered. Now that he was bedfast, it had hit him that the local gossips, like buzzards, would have a high old time after his death, and his children and grand-children (his wife had passed on) — who otherwise would remember him as a legendary hero — would soon be shocked to see an embarrassing part of his life that so far he had managed to keep in the shadows of the past.

His good name would be smeared by one small mistake — and one involving the death of a no-account drifter at that.

And after the many brave things he had done to keep the peace!

One of his favorite stories, in fact, was about how, shortly before he retired as sheriff, he collared Odie Wallace's boy in town one night. If anybody thought he was too old for his job, they sure didn't after that.

The boy, who was pretty husky, was drinking and acting smart-alecky. He had been bowed up for some time anyway because of all that talk that Sam had been messing with the kid's wife while she was waitressing down at the cafe. Well, young Wallace was plainly looking for trouble when he hesitated after being told to get off the street, and Sam never was fool enough to let another man make the first move. He laid that big kid out with one good blow to the temple.

From then on the boy was never quite right, and couldn't work — Odie and his wife wound up having to help take care of the boy's baby — and there was the usual kind of talk that Sam must have hit him with something other than his fist, but nobody important paid any attention to that.

Odie never got over it, of course. He was a churchgoer, but it was plain that he hated Sam like God hates sin. Once when they met on the street, Odie looked him straight in the eye and said, "I'm gonna try very hard to forgive you, Sam Dodson."

Sam just grinned — this was his favorite part of the story — and said he didn't give a damn about being forgiven.

But now, Sam faced something he couldn't laugh off, and feared he couldn't handle. The worry had become a gnawing demon inside him that spawned bad dreams day and night, then woke him with chills and sweats and set his heavy body to trembling so hard the bed springs creaked to nearly drown out the whir of the electric fan a few feet away.

Finally, he sent for his onetime cohort, Hooley Dills.

"How ya feelin', Sam? Can I bring ya anything?" Hooley said, taking a chair beside the bed.

"Yeah, you sure can," Sam said between coughs and belches. He glanced toward the bedroom door to make sure Blanche, his caretaker, was out of earshot. "Go down to the courthouse and swipe them old trial records — you know the ones. Then go into Linus Edwards' office and get what copies there are of the newspapers that printed anything about it. Not that Linus ever had sense enough to get things right, but he did report the case."

"Then burn all the damn stuff here in my backyard. That way, once the talk starts nobody can find any proof."

"Sam, I wouldn't worry about that. That was a long time ago, and them three guys who was with you out there in the woods that night are dead and gone, and most of the jurors and lawyers who had anything to do with the trial are, too."

"Besides," he said, "you bein' the sheriff then, most everybody trusted your judgement, and later figured like you did — even if that fella wasn't the one who beat that farmer to death, he was an ex-convict and probably did plenty of other things to be hung for. That musta been why the jury couldn't reach a verdict and it was a mistrial."

"And to this very day," he added, "I don't think anybody's ever really called it a lynchin'."

"Don't tell me not to worry! There's still some around who remember. And I know people in this county — while I'm alive they know better than to even whisper about me, but once I'm gone they'll be blabbin' their fool heads off. I bet they won't even wait till I'm covered up good."

"But Sam, stealin' court records is against the law, ain't it? And Linus will wanna know why I'm askin' about old newspapers. Besides, I'm sure all the papers dealin' with that case was sold out long ago, and Linus may not be very smart, but he don't let nobody have the old papers he keeps — you know, back in the place he calls his 'morgue.'"

"I don't give a damn! Now listen, everybody knows

you was my deputy for years, and they won't think anything about you roamin' around the court clerk's office. And you know Linus is dumb as a sow possum. Tell him you're lookin' up family history — old obituaries, such as that — and you oughta be able to tear a few pages out of his morgue papers without him noticin'."

Hooley was back the next day, beaming. "Well, I got the court records, Sam. And I snuck out with the old newspapers you wanted, too."

"Good! Now start a fire out back. I'll watch it through the window." Then he hollered toward the kitchen, from where the noontime smells further cheered him. "Blanche, ain't it about time to eat? And bring me some real food this time — not that damn watery chicken soup!"

"By the way, Linus Edwards was real obligin'," Hooley said. "In fact, after he asked me how you was, and when, like you said, I told him I was lookin' up old obituaries, he got a big idea: He's gonna do 'a full-page layout' in advance, and have it ready to run with your obit. He got plumb enthused — said it'll be all about you, and the biggest story he's ever done."

"Do what? A big story? What's that idiot up to anyway?" Sam coughed, then grabbed a nearby hand towel and blew his nose.

"Oh, I wouldn't worry about it, Sam. I asked him what all he's gonna say and he said he'll write about your 'long and distinguished career' as a lawman, and said he'll just barely mention that old trouble — he's even gonna say how you kept tryin' to find that farmer's real killer after being put through the ordeal of a trial and all."

Sam grunted.

Hooley was back a few days later, with more news. "Sam, I saw Linus Edwards this mornin' down at the cafe and he said people all over town have been talkin' about you and that old case. I guess one of the girls in the clerk's office mentioned it at the beauty shop or someplace that I was askin' about them old trial records. Funny how word spreads, ain't it? I'm just glad nobody seen me sneak the records out; I was extra careful."

"And you know, Sam," he added, "maybe Linus is smarter than we think. He said he told 'em I was helpin' him do research for his story about you. Then he told 'em all about the big full-page layout he's plannin' — and he said a lot of people sure perked up their ears about that."

Sam grunted.

Hooley was back the next day. "Sam, you know what? I saw Linus Edwards again this mornin' and he said some guy from The Associated Press called 'im, askin' about the big story he's plannin'. Ain't it funny how word spreads? Linus didn't know how the guy heard about it, but said that, bein' his paper is just a small weekly, he was glad to tell the AP guy all about his plans to honor you with his full-page spread — said that way he figured both you and the whole town will get nice publicity all over Oklahoma."

Sam grunted and mumbled something that Hooley didn't understand, and then Hooley went on. "Linus said the AP guy was interested in that old trial, and said he was surprised it didn't make bigger headlines than it did all over the whole state. I wouldn't worry about it, though, Sam. Linus said the guy was enthused about the 'colorful' part of it. Said he called it the biggest story since that time them four guys was strung up in the livery barn in Ada a few years after statehood — you know, them three local guys and that hired killer from Texas."

Hooley grinned. "And Linus said the guy was real enthused about revivin' all that stuff and writin' about what he called this 'Old West history.'"

Sam pushed aside his unfinished plate of fried chicken, mashed potatoes, mustard greens and cornbread, choking a little on the last mouthful and sputtering his buttermilk.

A few days later, Hooley was back. Sam wasn't especially glad to see him, but Hooley told him the latest anyway. "Ya know, Sam, them big-city reporters ask a lot more questions than Linus does, and I guess they have ways of diggin' up more information than he can. Anyway, seems like that AP guy is doin' a lot more research about you than necessary — but maybe that's because he don't know you real well like Linus does and has to start from scratch."

Hooley went on to say the AP reporter told Linus Edwards he was studying the former sheriff's complete background — including the sheriff being tried after the suspect in the farmer's killing was hanged from a tree; how the suspect's alibi later checked out; plus the fact that the farmer was also chairman of the county election board, and had been scheduled to testify before a grand jury, apparently about "alleged voting irregularities" in a close sheriff's race.

"Linus said he remembered all that, of course, but since the election board chairman didn't live to testify, and since the grand jury didn't do anything official except recommend the jail be cleaned up, he didn't write much about it — especially since he wasn't anxious to give the town bad publicity anyhow."

Sam snorted, and Hooley continued. "But Linus says the AP guy thinks the farmer got killed when someone came to talk to 'im, and the discussion turned into an argument, then worse. The AP guy said the medical examiner's report showed the farmer was hit with a heavy object — like maybe a pistol. And the AP guy thinks the case could even be revived, and they might catch the killer yet — that is, if he's still alive, of course."

Sam groaned and pulled the sheet over his face.

"Linus said the AP guy is comin' to town tomorrow and interview people — said he wanted to get 'comments,' from everybody who wants to talk to 'im. He said he's gonna interview you, in fact — well, naturally, he would since you're the one Linus' big story is all about."

Sam coughed and gagged, and Hooley called out for Blanche. After she helped Sam lean over so he could heave into the slop jar, then washed his face and gave him a pill and glass of water, Hooley went on. "The AP guy told Linus he was sure grateful somebody from here called 'im, other-

---

wise he would've missed the whole story. Said the one who called 'im wouldn't give his name — the guy called 'im 'anonymous' — but that when he called he just said that he heard there was going to be a big story about the sheriff, and that he wanted to make sure some things were included in it."

Hooley frowned, then went on. "I don't know why somebody from around here wouldn't just tell Linus to begin with, instead of makin' a long-distance call to some outsider, do you, Sam?

"And something else — the guy said just before the caller hung up he said something like 'I'm gonna try very hard to forgive myself for telling you this.' Funny thing for somebody to say, wasn't it?"

Sam closed his eyes and emitted a long, low moan.

Hooley hushed, thinking the time had come for his former boss, but after a moment went on. "Anyhow, Sam, I wouldn't worry about all this. Some of that AP guy's talk sounds pretty farfetched to me."

"Besides," he said, "I told Linus, let the guy come ahead on, that you ain't got nothin' to hide. And you sure ain't afraid of some young big-city reporter that's still wet behind the ears. Just like you wasn't afraid to be a lawman all them years, and to put up with that ordeal of a trial and all."

"In fact, Sam," Hooley stood up to add, "me and Linus agreed, most everybody around here knows you're the toughest man in this whole county. And if anybody don't know it, they will after all this publicity gets out. Why, after you're gone, they'll be talkin' about you for years to come."

On Friday, May 26, 1978, in the vicinity of Kenefic and Caddo, a shoot-out between three Oklahoma Highway Patrolmen and two escaped prisoners left the three lawmen – Lt. Pat Grimes and troopers Billy Young and Houston "Pappy" Summers — and both escapees – Claude Dennis and Michael Lancaster — dead. This story is based on that tragedy, as well as the legend of Belle Starr's ghost.

Escape!

"If any cops show up behind us, let 'em have it!" Brassfield, his eyes fixed on the two-lane, yelled at me over the grind of the motor and the howl of hot air through the open windows. And he threw in a bunch of dirty words.

In all my years off and on behind bars, I never took up the profane talk common among cons. I guess when you were raised by an old-fashioned country preacher, some things just stick with you. Like my feelings about death. I never believed exactly what I was taught, but I've always felt like there was *something* after you die. And I had come to think that, whatever it was, it couldn't be worse than prison.

Now, though, I not only wished I was back in my cell – I had decided death had to be better than being on the run with someone like Red Brassfield.

"We're okay, Red," I yelled, but kept looking back like he told me, while praying I wouldn't have to use the thirty-eight. Of all the things I'd done, I had never killed anyone, and didn't know if I could.

Praying was something else that had stuck with me, even if I hadn't done much of it since I was a kid. Except for the last few hours.

Brassfield was every bit as bad as his talk. He was in for murder and rape, and after he got in prison choked a cellmate to death. He had somehow dodged the chair, but had so many convictions there was only one way he would ever get out of Big Mac.

Which is what he had just done. And he schemed things so that I was on the same work detail and could go over the fence with him. I knew better than to tell him no.

We had made our way to a pawnshop, and took a couple of guns and the owner's car. I wanted to tie the guy up, but Brassfield slit his throat.

"Dead men stay nice and quiet, right?" he had said, and grinned real big.

We were now several miles southwest of McAlester and heading toward the state line, where Brassfield said we would ditch the car, cross into Texas, then split up.

But I knew that, once at the river, he wouldn't need me anymore, and I kept seeing the poor guy in the pawnshop. I had to get away from Red Brassfield soon, but couldn't figure how.

We were nearing the small town up ahead. "Okay, you used to live around this hick place, right? Tell me where to go," Brassfield said. That was why he had brought me along.

I told him. We would go through town, then take a few dirt roads I knew that would take us all the way to the Red River. There, we could hide the car in the willows and swim cross.

"You better be right!" he snapped. "I don't aim to get lost somewhere out in the sticks."

It was warm in the late afternoon, and the town's main street sunny — and deserted except for a girl strolling and sipping a Coke. She would have stood out on the streets of New York City. She was maybe seventeen, her expression cute and bright, her blonde hair in pony tails, her blouse full

Thunder in the Heartland

and bouncy, and from white socks and athletic shoes up to short skirt her legs were a mouth-watering color and just starting to look womanly.

Probably the local star cheerleader, I thought. And I knew exactly what Brassfield was thinking.

"Saaay, maybe we oughta take a hostage with us, right? Wonder if she's ever parked by the river?" His grin had a nasty curl to it.

"You're gonna take the wheel," he said, pulling to the curb a little ahead of the girl. "I'll get out and go around and stop her, like I'm askin' directions. Then I'll grab her. Soon as I have her between us, you drive on."

I knew I couldn't change his mind, but tried anyway. "Red, don't ya think ... I mean, we cause any commotion and the law will be on us in a second. Don't ya think we better get on to the river? I mean, I'm just worried that . . . . "

"Shut up! I know how to keep 'em quiet. When we're through, we'll leave her with the car. Now slide over and take the wheel!" He opened the door and got out.

My heart pounded the same way it did when I saw what was about to happen to the guy in the pawnshop. I wished I

Investigators at the scene of the fatal gun battle. Copyright 1978, The Oklahoma Publishing Company.

---

could do something. I thought about jumping out and letting Brassfield have it with the thirty-eight, then throwing up my hands and waiting on the cops. But I couldn't do anything but sit there — and hope the girl would have sense enough to run.

She didn't, though. She just stopped and twisted around and flashed a big red smile and waited as he came toward her. I looked away, and prayed again.

A car with a big star on the door pulled up about a block past the four-way stop — probably the local police officer taking his regular watch for speeders. I let out a deep breath.

Brassfield saw the cop, too, and got back in. He cussed a bunch, but eased the car back into the street and drove on.

Later, from the dirt road, I looked out at the trees that were leafed out real pretty and thought of the picnics my parents used to take on Sunday afternoons after church. Happy memories, of times before I grew up and started making mistakes, like stealing, which got to be a habit.

"I hear your old man was a preacher," Brassfield said — he must have known I was thinking of home the way I was gazing out the window. "I guess you believe in Heaven and hell, right?" He grinned, the way he did when he was trying to pick a fight.

I thought of how my dad, back before TV, used to tell me stories after supper — ghost stories, because he knew I liked them. Him being a minister, he explained that he didn't believe in ghosts, of course, but told the stories just for fun. And I remembered my favorite.

It was then that, without really planning, I started talking about it — I guess I figured it would keep Brassfield calm till we got to the river, and maybe improve my chances of getting away from him.

"That makes me think, Red. You've heard of Belle Starr, the famous woman outlaw? Well, there's a story, right here in this part of the country, about Belle Starr's ghost. Ever hear it?"

"You kiddin' me?" He narrowed his eyes and looked

at me like I had called him stupid, and added a few bad words. But he sounded curious, so I went on.

They say down close to Younger's Bend, up a ways from the Canadian River, where Belle Starr used to live and close to where she was shot and killed by someone — on the night of a full moon, she comes out, galloping toward you on her horse. And she's calling out something, over and over.

"And what's that?"

"Well, some people say she's tryin' to tell who killed her — it never was known who shot her." I kept thinking and talking, trying to remember all the story, and make up stuff where I couldn't. "But some say she's tryin' to tell whoever will listen that she's sorry for any wrong she did, and that...."

"You believe that? When you're dead you're dead! I oughta know — I never seen anyone that I killed come back yet!" He laughed, like he had said something clever. But I knew he was still interested.

"And she keeps calling and calling, and...."

I could tell by the mesquite growth in the pastures that we were getting close to the river. That's when I looked behind us, and saw a tiny cloud of road dust. I turned back, and up ahead and off to the left was more dust — another car was about to head us off at a crossroads.

Brassfield saw it, too. "There they come!" he yelled, spewing bad words. "That hick cop back in town probably seen us — somebody musta broadcast the tag number." He stomped on the gas, and pulled the forty-five semiautomatic from his belt. By now we could hear sirens.

Before I knew it, we had pulled into a ditch and were both outside and crouched behind the car, twisting and ducking while Brassfield was shooting at the two highway patrol cars that had stopped, several yards away at separate positions. And three or four patrolmen were firing back, their slugs whacking into our car from different angles — the noise so deafening I could barely hear Brassfield screaming cuss words.

I knew it was too late — to either get away from Brassfield or give myself up. If I tried to surrender, if the patrolmen didn't gun me down, Brassfield would the second he saw me stand up. There was no place for me to go. I had never felt so trapped, and so alone, not even in prison. I almost wished . . . .

Something jolted me in the shoulder, knocking me down. When I tried to move, my whole left side was numb.

Finally, I sat up, and looked over at Brassfield. Things were blurry, but I could see he was taking aim at a patrolman who was already on the ground near one of the cars, and was bleeding and trying to crawl back out of the line of fire.

I wasn't sure whether I was actually doing it, or was dreaming, but I remember aiming the thirty-eight at Brassfield's head, then pulling the trigger a second after he turned and looked at me, his eyes wide and his mouth open. I don't think he had time to say a bad word.

I stood up, dropping my pistol, but immediately felt another jolt, this time in my chest. I fell hard on my back — but amazingly, I didn't hurt, not anywhere.

In fact, I had never felt so good, and never understood things so clearly, despite the sudden change of scene — I must have dozed briefly.

There were more people around, and the uniformed men walking toward me seemed friendly, like the whole world at this strange moment. I knew, somehow, no one would harm me, just as I knew I would never harm anyone, or do anything wrong again. I thought again of my dad, and mother too, both long dead, and how I wanted to tell them I loved them, and was sorry for all my mistakes — but that I was now at peace, with the world, and with myself.

Suddenly, I *had* to tell them — and anyone else who would listen. So I smiled and spoke to the officers as they walked up to me. They didn't seem to hear me, though, not even when they came closer and covered me with a clean, cool sheet that felt good to my face.

But I took it off and got up — it was so easy and painless to move. I really couldn't remember ever feeling so wonderful. Except, that is, for my frustrated efforts to communicate with someone.

But I'm not worried. I'll keep calling and calling. And sooner or later, someone will hear me.

For years the Old Day County Reunion, a folksy July get-together, has been held at the far western Oklahoma site of Grand, once a town in Oklahoma Territory times. It's also the site of only one grave, and no one can say for sure who's in it – maybe Harry Leslie, maybe William Latta, or somebody else. The mystery has spawned some wild tales, like this one.

Old-Timers' Reunion

Clint Davis hesitated after tying his horse with the others, then walked toward the big shade tree and water hole and the happy sounds — people talking and laughing, music, and youngsters shrieking and splashing.

Like other men of his kind, Davis shied from crowds, and normally wouldn't even stop to refill his canteen and water his horse at such a time. Now, though, something lured him. Possibly it was the rich smell of barbecued beef, and the promise of a cool rest under the giant, ancient cottonwood near the spring-fed pool — a spot that would look heavenly to most any traveler on this hot afternoon.

But he was badgered by an odd feeling. Not so much a forewarning of danger — something to which he was long inured — but a tingling, a man might call it. As always, he would be wary.

"Howdy, Clint. I figured you'd show up." The voice came from behind, and Davis drew and cocked his forty-five as he wheeled — then saw there was no threat, but nevertheless received a shock.

"Slim Goodall!" Clint recognized the man, despite the tired eyes and creased face that weren't there before, then had to regain his wits. "I thought you was dead! Thought you got strung up a few years back after some holdup down by the Red River. I musta heard wrong."

Through a worn look of sadness, Goodall managed a grin. "I heard somethin' like that about you. The talk was, a Texas Ranger got ya over in the Panhandle."

"What the hell you talkin' about? The day some damn lawman is big enough to corral Clint Davis, you'll know about it! And how come you was expectin' me? I hadn't been by this place in a year or more. I wouldn't have stopped today if I'd known some church picnic was goin' on, or whatever this is."

"It's a reunion, mostly of old-timers. They get together here every summer. It started around a hundred years ago. Things have changed, of course. Some still come horseback, but most folks get here other ways." As they walked, he glanced off to where the sun struck the metal tops of numerous odd-looking vehicles, left side by side in row upon row.

"This place ain't like I remember, true enough. And *you* sure ain't makin' much sense, Goodall. I'd say you had too much to drink, except it appears all they got at this crazy get-together is lemonade and such."

They had approached the tables, covered with white cloths and lined on one side by ladies waiting to serve the barbecue and other vittles — pork roast, chicken, potatoes and gravy, cooked greens, salads, pie and cake, and watermelon.

"That old man playin' the fiddle, that's Guy Hammond." Goodall indicated one of four men on a makeshift stage. "He owns this place now."

"What? You're crazy!" Clint dropped his voice to a frenzied whisper. "I killed Guy Hammond about two years ago — I was robbing the bank in Cheyenne, and he come from

---

behind the counter with a gun. I shot 'im dead in his tracks!"

Goodall's answer was matter-of-fact. "That was George Hammond, the banker. He was Guy's daddy — and it was longer ago than you thought. Guy here, he's always farmed and run cattle. You might recall, years ago this was part of the Lafferty Ranch, the biggest outfit in the Territory until it was broken up and sold off after statehood. Lafferty's always been a big name here, you know. H.C. Lafferty — the old man, the one who homesteaded here — he built the first church and school in these parts."

Clint spoke in low tones again. "I never heard about the ranch bein' sold, but I sure remember that name. I shot it out with one of the Laffertys after he nearly put me in jail — claimed I was maverick-brandin' some of his calves. Guess I should've paid a lawyer like Temple Houston to get me out of it, but instead I went to Lafferty's place and called 'im out. Afterwards, I went in his house and took what cash I could find to pay for my trouble, then high-tailed it."

"Fact is," he said, "this is my first time back to this country since. I gave it about a year to blow over."

"It took a little longer than that. That was H.C.'s younger brother. I heard about it — everybody did. Especially about him bein' found shot in the back — it wasn't no shoot-out — and about you goin' in his house, and how you had your way with his wife."

"You know a lot about me, don't ya? And I ain't sure I like the way you're talkin', Goodall. If you're funnin' me, you better be damn careful!"

Goodall smiled — in his usual dismal way, but calmly, which puzzled Clint. At one time this same man would cringe before him in a second.

"And tell me, Goodall, what are *you* doin' here anyhow?"

"Oh, I can get out to places like this once in a while — just enough for me to know what I'm missin'. It'll probably be the same with you."

"What in hell you talkin' about?"

"You'll find out for yourself — just like you found your way here today."

"Me? I just happened to ride by." Clint frowned to himself. "Leastwise, I guess I did. I don't remember exactly — with the heat, maybe I dozed in the saddle."

"Anyhow, the grub looks good, don't it?" he said as he and Goodall got in line. Someone was mumbling a long prayer.

As their plates were heaped, and while every server smiled and greeted them, Clint was filled with happiness by the convivial affair, and a gushing love for these simple, unselfish people. He found he couldn't stop talking. He went on and on — even, for the first time, speaking openly about himself. After all, he, too, had returned home, and had to share his wonderful new feelings. "Thank you, ma'am. I'm Clint Davis. I grew up around here. I been away, but you musta heard of me, and you must know my folks. I'm . . . ."

All of them, though, returned his comments with courteous but blank expressions, their eyes full of friendliness, but not recognition.

Later, he and Goodall, their stomachs full, sat by the green pool, and Clint looked up, through the flickering green and yellow leaves of the cottonwood at patches of blue sky and puffy white clouds. He felt daydreamy.

"Ya know," he said, "I never thought this would happen, but somethin's come over me since I rode in here today. It's somethin' about this place – it's different from the last time I was here. It's prettier, I guess."

"That's right, it is different," Goodall said.

"And I never knew I'd like bein' among decent people like these. Startin' today, I ain't the man I used to be. And I never saw such a beautiful day – this is the greatest day of my life!"

He thought then of the servers. "'Course, the people ain't used to me yet, I guess, since every time I talk to 'em, they look at me funnylike. It's almost like they're lookin' right through me — like, in a way, I ain't even here. Like no matter what I say, they can't hear me.

"Fact is, Goodall, if *you* wasn't here, I guess *nobody* could hear me."

"That's right," Goodall said.

"So you're the only one who can help me – you can help me talk to these people."

"I can't," Goodall said. "They don't hear me, either."

They started walking again, this time away from the gathering, but Clint was too troubled to notice the direction.

They came upon a low mound, resembling a grave, but weedy and unmarked.

"Is somebody buried there?" Clint said.

"That's right. Has been for years," Goodall said. "The talk is, it was an outlaw, planted out here all by hisself instead of in a proper cemetery, with decent folks — such a bad hombre that he wasn't even fit for boot hill."

He added: "But didn't you know that already? I figured that's why you come here in the first place, to see the grave."

"What?" Clint stared at Goodall, turned to study the grave again, and became more flustered. "Who *is* buried here, anyhow?"

"You mean you don't know?"

"Goodall, how the hell *would* I know? And I've had enough of your crazy talk!" His anger flared, and he grabbed his forty-five and wheeled.

But Goodall was gone.

The sun was lowering and the crowd breaking up, and Clint Davis, the blissful feeling now gone, moved aside as several people, still talking and laughing, strode past.

He watched as they walked over the grave. It was like the damn people didn't even see it.

The fictional setting here is Tulsa, which has been described as one of America's most beautiful cities. It's where a story about art, and romance, seems to fit.

A Pretty Picture

Sylvia took a deep breath. "Yes, Mother, I *know* most girls my age are married, and that I'll probably never find my 'dream man'! It's simply that I'd rather stay single than settle for second best – like I almost did once. Call me an idealist, but I'll wait for the perfect guy. Even if he never comes along."

She knew word for word what her mother was going to say.

"But Sylvia dear, you don't want to spend the rest of your life alone. And Fred is such a fine young man — so intelligent, so mannerly. Good-looking, too. And it's obvious he adores you."

"And I've told you, Mother, Fred is a very dear friend. But that's all he is. There's no ... Well, there's no excitement — no *magic*, you might call it — between us. At least, not on my part. You see, it's like my profession. For me to do a painting, I have to be inspired. The *inspiration* — the *magic* — has to be there."

"Besides," she added, "until my artwork starts selling – the kind of art I really want to do – I'm too busy to even think about marriage. My ad agency has been doing so well that I'm much too occupied — more than I'd like to be, really."

Sylvia had explained her feelings to her mother so many times she knew she was right. Well, almost knew.

She had to admit she got lonely, and envisioned coming home to the ideal husband, and telling him all about her day – maybe after painting the most beautiful landscape ever of the Tulsa skyline — then relaxing in front of the TV, her head on his shoulder. And occasionally they would go out for dinner and give each other rapturous looks over candlelight.

She wasn't sure what he would be like, but he was always the same handsome and charming man who had been in her dreams since childhood.

Also, she recalled how happy her parents had seemed while she was growing up. Their middle-class home was in one of the city's most wooded and picturesque neighborhoods – where she decided as a girl to become an artist. Her father had long since died, but her mother often fondly reminisced about their marriage.

The next day at noon, Fred, as he often did, stopped by Sylvia's office. "Got time for lunch?" he asked, in his pleasant — but predictable — way.

They had met in college. While their goals differed — she studied art; he majored in business — they instantly struck a rapport; it was like they had known each other always. Their companionship grew, and she even found herself depending upon his advice and moral support.

Once, his kind and understanding words even helped her overcome a traumatic broken engagement to someone else — who had proved unfaithful. That had nearly been a tragic mistake. She had convinced herself she was making the right decision and accepted his engagement ring — when in her heart she knew he wasn't the man she had always dreamed about.

So she had promised herself she would be sure next time — if there were a next time.

She often wished she really felt something for Fred, as he clearly did for her. But she could only see him as a wonderful friend. They had met and talked often during the past three years — as *buddies*. The only time they dated — and she didn't call it that — was occasionally when she and her mother invited him to a home-cooked meal. Which, of course, was always her mother's idea.

"Still getting more clients than you can handle?" he said when they were eating in the crowded food court of the mall a short drive from her agency.

"Really! I'll tell you, Fred, at first I was thrilled that my little agency even survived, but now it's about to devour me. I can't handle the business end of it, all the paperwork."

"Well, Sylvia, like I've told you, you need a business partner — and it so happens I know just the right one!" He gave her an exaggerated rakish grin.

"I'm *sure* you do. Actually, though, Fred, my real problem is doing the designs and ad layouts, believe it or not. I know I'm supposed to be a commercial artist, but I simply don't like it. And I spend so much time forcing myself to do that kind of work for my clients that I get behind with the books - which I hate even more!"

She leaned forward and, without fully realizing it, continued to unload laments that Fred had heard over and over. "I want to be a painter. I want to paint simple but enchanting scenes, like the Boston Avenue Methodist Church at dawn, the Will Rogers Memorial at Claremore, even Western settings in Osage County. I want to express myself."

She set down her cup, loudly. "I may never be known, like such people as Charles Banks Wilson and the late sculptor Willard Stone, and my paintings probably will never hang in Gilcrease or Philbrook, but I have to do what inspires me.

My work has to have that certain *magic*. I've got to *feel* something about what I do."

"I know, I know. But seriously, Sylvia, I can help you. I can set up your books so you'll have substantially more time for your commercial designs. And that way you'll have more time for the type of art you like, until you get established as a painter – which I believe someday you'll do. But first you have to solve a few business problems – and that's what *I'm* good at doing."

He placed his hand on hers. "Tell you what, let's discuss it over dinner tonight. My boss has been talking about a new Italian place. He said the food and atmosphere are sensational, and . . . ."

"Fred, I've told you, dinner isn't like lunch. If I had dinner with you, that would be like ... Well, you know. I just don't think it's a good idea. I'm sorry." She removed his hand.

She saw the flick of hurt in his brown eyes, but as usual he was understanding. "Sylvia, I know how you feel, but there's nothing wrong with mixing a little pleasure with business. Tell you what, I'll remember we're just good friends and promise not to propose, at least not with a mouthful of spaghetti!"

He usually ended such talks with a humorous note – one of his qualities she loved – but she was firm. "No, Fred. I know you're sincere about wanting to help me, and you're so sweet that way, but it wouldn't be fair for me to encourage you. Like I've said before, let's not ruin a great friendship. Okay?"

A few days later he stopped by her office when he saw the light was still on after closing time. She was fuming over her drawing board.

"Fred, I simply don't have time to talk right now!" she said without looking up. "I was so behind with invoices and bills, I had to put off doing all these designs. And the deadline for them is tomorrow!"

"And here's the worst part." She stood and threw down her pencil. "Just look at this sketch — it looks like something a child would do! Fred, I've just discovered that I can't work under pressure. I'm a good artist, but only when I have time to get inspired. I can't produce professional work in a hurry — and that's what a commercial artist has to do. I'm a total failure!" Her voice broke.

"But, Sylvia, you're a fine artist." He took her by the shoulders. "You see, even though this commercial art isn't what you like to do, you do most of it without waiting for inspiration. What happens is, you actually *force* yourself to get inspired — and your sketches are good, even if you don't think so. You probably don't know it, but you've been doing that ever since you started this agency last year. Otherwise, your business wouldn't be such a success.

"You're just overwhelmed right now because you're so far behind. And that, incidentally, is only because you won't let me help you!"

He was right! She *had* turned out good sketches time after time, and she *had* felt at least some inspiration, even when under pressure — but hadn't realized that until Fred told her.

"Oh, Fred, thank you! And I'm sorry I was rude to you. I don't know what on earth I would ever do without you!"

"Well, lady, that's exactly what I've been trying to tell you for about three years now!"

Sylvia smiled as she swept away a tear with the back of her hand. She felt like a little girl. "Fred, you're the only person in the world who could make me laugh at a time like this. You're the most wonderful man I know."

"Hey, getting a little carried away, aren't you? But don't stop!"

She laughed again — and in the same instant she saw something for the first time, though for at least a year it had been as plain as one of her designs on the drawing board.

Like she herself had said, romance was like inspiration — the magic had to be there. But now she knew that sometimes an artist had to *develop* inspiration, as she had been doing at her agency.

So maybe romance, like inspiration, required a little work – or creativity.

She looked up at him again. Her mother was right! He *was* good-looking. Maybe he was even right about a part-nership — but she wasn't thinking solely about business. She couldn't wait to tell her mother about her new feelings.

But only after she told Fred he was the man of her dreams.

On Wednesday, April 19, 1995, a few minutes after 9 a.m., a bomb tore apart the Alfred P. Murrah Building in Oklahoma City, leaving the "Heartland" – a term almost immediately entrenched into the Oklahoma vocabulary, and thereafter cherished -- with a wound that would never heal. This story is about an imaginary decent human being who, like the 168 real victims, didn't deserve to die this way,

Thunder in the Heartland

Robert Updike stepped from his car into the quiet shade of the residential district and caught the freshness of the morning air. He immediately was reminded of his boyhood — which should be a joyful memory.

Robert was on his way to his CPA's office, and had parked several blocks away in the older, wooded neighborhood that fringed the downtown area. He had phoned his secretary at the oil company that he would come in late. He didn't mind the walk.

He had filed for an extension when he knew he would miss the April 15 deadline, but still was eager to get his income tax material sent off. He and Barbara expected a nice refund, and would use it for landscaping their home. They had gradually beautified the place since building it several years ago, and some nice trees would be the final touch in making it a showplace a few years from now.

That's when his life would be at a nice plateau. He and Barbara would be enjoying his retirement — if it weren't spoiled by this thing about his health. And by then Susan should be out of college and on her own. But he had some concerns there, too, even if Barbara thought he worried for nothing.

"Oh, Robert, she'll do all right," she had said over their coffee that morning. "Her grades aren't all that bad, really. You're such a perfectionist — you know, you're like your dad, that way."

"That's not true, Barbara! I only want her to do what she's capable of. And take life a little more seriously."

"Don't shout! I'm sorry. I shouldn't have mentioned your father. I keep forgetting about this hang-up of yours. Actually, I still don't understand your feelings. You're not the only child to come from a broken home, you know. And he at least provided well for his family, and saw that you were grown, before he ... Well, before he did what he did. Besides, he isn't the first old married man to develop a roving eye."

Robert stood up. His chair scraped the floor. "I can't believe you said that! You know how terrible that was for my mother."

"Yes, I do. And that was tragic. But maybe you're more upset about what he did to *you* — I'm sure it was a dreadful embarrassment. But why not forget it? You have your own family. Besides, I still say older men sometimes do those things — even men who live in big, fine houses in quiet little towns."

She looked down and smiled as she stirred her coffee. "Of course, I'm not worried about *you*, my dear. You're too square."

"I don't know why you brought this up!" he said. "I'm going to work."

As Robert drove along the interstate, he was aware again of the tightness in his lower back. The urologist had said it was his prostate, and that something called his PSA was high, and had strongly suggested a biopsy. He wouldn't mention it to Barbara until it was necessary, if it ever were. He would decide about the biopsy later.

It was hard to believe how simple his life once was.

Robert had grown up in a tiny community where his father owned the general store. It was a place where he and other youngsters spent summers playing in quiet streets and in yards fronted with rose bushes and shaded by elm and silver maple trees; where they drank nickel soda pop in the tiny business district and never lacked for fun even before black-and-white television. It was the model of small-town America — an idyllic little world of its own where every day was a page out of a Norman Rockwell calendar, and where time had been kind enough to stop for a while.

But it was also a place where scandals weren't supposed to happen. Especially scandals involving intelligent, dignified and dedicated fathers — like the one he thought he knew.

Robert was home after his first year of college when the affair between his father, who was on the School Board, and the young, pretty art teacher came to light — at least, for Robert and his mother. It had already provided amusement for the rest of the town for several weeks.

"Wonder where Mister Updike's at?" one of the regular loafers said to another one day when Robert was helping in the store. He was crouched behind the counter opening a box of canned tomatoes. His father was in the back showing a customer some plow points.

"Beats me," the other man said. "But if the schoolhouse wasn't closed for summer, I'd have a pretty good guess."

Robert stood still as both men laughed. His face tingled. They stared back, their eyes wide and their grins clabbered, then hurriedly left.

That had been during the few days of turmoil — the awkward interim during which he, and especially his mother, were trying to adjust to the crisis and planning how

to react. Robert recalled there had long been a polite tense-
ness between his parents that at the time he barely noticed,
but that didn't change his feelings. After he helped his
mother move, he left his hometown for good. And he promised his father he would never see him again.

His mother got practically everything in the divorce.
She sold both their home and the store, and then moved to a
retirement area on Eufaula Lake where her brother and his
wife lived. She had always liked visiting them there. Robert
and Barbara went to see her regularly.

His father had stayed in town after the breakup, buy-
ing a small house and living alone. The teacher moved away.

His mother seemed to be adjusting well enough to a
new life of her own — but then was killed when her car
went off the road one night when she was driving home
from a bingo party. There was no doubt in Robert's mind
what happened. His father might as well have been at the
wheel.

A few years later, his father died. Robert got a call that
he had fallen in his yard one icy morning while taking water to the birds. He was dead by the time neighbors got him
to a hospital. Doctors said it was a heart attack.

Robert handled the arrangements and got through the
graveside service on the cold, windy hill, avoiding the con-
dolences and handshaking as best he could. Within minutes,
he sped away, through what was left of the dusty little community.

For years his father had been the quintessential family
man, and was determined that his son get the best education possible. But he also was a nature lover, and regularly
took Robert hunting and fishing. It was his penchant for the
outdoors and the earth in general that inspired Robert to
study geology.

"This is my favorite place to look at the leaves this time
of year," he said one crisp day many years ago. It was during one of their jaunts in the country, and they had sat down
among several tall trees. "Most of these are cottonwood, but

---

these with the white bark, they're sycamore — and that's the prettiest tree, I think. It has those big leaves that show a lot of color, especially in the fall."

"Sounds like that's your favorite tree, huh, Dad?" Robert was more interested in the chance to rest for a while. They had walked for miles, up and down hills, through tall, scratchy weeds and over rocks and rough ground.

"Well, I guess so. But there are lots of others that are pretty, too. Like the redbud, for one — that's the state tree. Did you know that?"

His father looked up. "And you know, there's just the right time to see the full color of autumn leaves — when the weather's just right, and on just the right day, and maybe just the right moment. It's a time when the colors are at their peak — when there's no other moment like it. Then the leaves will start falling. And in a few days the pretty season will be over. Then winter will be here."

"Yeah, but after that, it'll be spring. And we can go fishin', can't we?"

"That's right. Spring's a nice time of year, too. But our weather is known for changing quick in the spring."

Robert's fatigue was forgotten, and he changed the subject. "Dad, you think we'll see something to shoot at before we go home?"

"Well, we'll do a little practicing before we get back to the car — I know a dead tree that'll make a nice target. We'll see it right after we cross over the hill."

"Oh, I forgot about that hill — we've sure walked a lot today, haven't we? I don't know how you can walk so much without getting tired."

"Oh, I get tired quicker than I used to. I always have liked to stop and rest in this spot, though, tired or not. I've stopped here and looked at the leaves many times — back when I used to hunt by myself, before you were born."

"Gosh, I bet there were bears and all kinds of wild animals here then."

"Well, not too many bears." His father had a way of

almost smiling. "But things do change over the years. In fact, we'd better not rest here too long. We might fall asleep, and be like ol' Rip Van Winkle."

"Who's that, Dad?"

"You don't know the story of Rip Van Winkle? He went hunting, then sat down and took a nap — then woke up years and years later, and he couldn't believe how everything had changed."

"That isn't true, though, is it?"

"Well, in a way it is. Life changes, whether we're ready for it to or not. And Change can be both good and bad. It's like these leaves – they die, but that makes the trees pretty in the fall. "

Robert heard a rapid thudding, and looked high up and spotted a colorful bird clinging to the side of a tree, its beak hammering into the trunk. He grabbed his four-ten shotgun, but his father raised a hand.

"No, no, son! Remember, you only kill what you're going to clean and take home and eat. Besides, that's a red-cockaded woodpecker. He's not only pretty, he's rare. This may be the only time you'll ever see one."

The bird flew off as a gust of wind came. It made a lonesome sound in the treetops and turned a picture-still canopy of bright and soft hues of yellow, orange, brown and crimson into a dry downpour of foliage. Robert looked up as the millions of crisp leaves fell around them, bringing the full, clean smell of autumn. They flickered in the cool sunlight before settling to the earth.

"Well, that's it — winter's on its way," his father said. "We'd better go. We don't want to sit here too long, and be like ol' Rip Van Winkle."

They looked at each other and grinned.

All that was before Robert learned of his father's other side. And before he resolved to leave it all in the past — his father, along with his halcyon boyhood.

The tightness in his lower back returned. It awakened his worry, and he knew it affected his stride — it wasn't long ago that he prided himself on how well and how far he could walk. Of course, the doctor had said that it could be simply an enlargement, which could be treated much easier than cancer. Enlargement was something natural, he said. It occurred in every man as the body changed. He suggested the biopsy as a precaution, but . . . .

Change.

The realization would have been humorous except for the deep despair. The seasons kept revolving. There was no such thing as a plateau in time. He had made himself the victim of an illusion. What he had been viewing with great anticipation for years could be only a mirage!

A breeze stirred in the leaves overhead. The freshness of the air, the earth around him, dappled with sunshine and shade, the *feeling* of nature — it was near enough to a day when the woods are in color, winds moan in the tree-tops, and there's the subtle blend of melancholia and bliss of autumn.

Robert had never known his father, or himself, as he did this minute.

What he had hated the man for the most was that he *couldn't* hate him, and what had pained him so was recalling the look in his father's eyes the last time they saw each other. It had been easier for him to feel anger than guilt. He had been slow to understand what his father tried to teach him — that life is seldom as beautiful, or as ugly, as it appears.

And that it should be lived in the present, even when it takes courage.

For the first time since he was in his teens, Robert longed to revisit his hometown. He would do that soon — after he saw the doctor again. For now, though, he would look forward to landscaping his yard. He quickened his step. He could walk for miles.

He had reached the downtown district, and the CPA's office was a couple of blocks ahead.

He passed in front of the federal building, and heard

thunder. He hadn't noticed any clouds, but storms came quickly this time of year.

After all, his dad would say, it was springtime in Oklahoma. He smiled to himself. The thunder turned deafening.

Five years after the explosion – which within minutes had become known as the deadliest domestic terrorist attack in America — people came daily to where a national monument had just been dedicated.

Many of them, though, were more impressed by personal notes from relatives of the people killed — mostly pieces of paper fastened to a fence. They fluttered in light breezes, and some were hand-printed and childlike. But all were heavy with feeling.

"They were just people," a woman said one day of the victims. "Average, decent people with daily worries and troubles — people just like us."

"Look at this one," said the woman with her. "A letter from someone's daughter. Listen to this part."

She read it: "For you, Dad, I graduated on the honor roll. And Mother and I have planted a tree for you in the yard — a sycamore, the kind you talk about so much. As it grows more beautiful every year, we'll know it's you."

"Sad, isn't it?" the other said. "Heaven only knows the story behind that one."

Afterword

It's been said that any writer's favorite book is the one he's working on at the moment. I certainly felt that way about this one — but may never stop feeling that way. That's because this collection reflects virtually every one of my experiences and observations worth remembering, as well as every fantasy, joy, sorrow, yearning and regret I ever had. In short, it's just about everything I have to say.

So after this is published, if I'm called Up Yonder before I write another line, I'll go with a grin.

JME

Index of Real Names